ENGLISH G

access 6

WORKBOOK

W0215155

Vokabel Trainer

Cornelsen

Vokabeltrainer-App

Verfügbar für: iOS, Android und Windows Phone

scook

AUDIOS online

Deine **interaktiven Gratis-Übungen** und **Audios** findest du auf scook.de. Dort gibst du den unten stehenden Zugangscode in die Box ein.

Dein Zugangscode auf www.scook.de | t9hos-yxf9g

Cornelsen

Who are you?

Die interaktive Übung 1 findest du auf www.scook.de. Zum Einloggen auf Scook brauchst du den Code auf Seite 1.

1

1 Profile photos ➜ SB (pp. 10–11) • Wordbank 1

In your exercise book, describe the people in the profile photos. How do you think they want others to see them? Which person would you prefer to be friends with, and why?

- *Photo 1 shows ...*
- *He is dressed ...*
- *Photo 2 looks as if it was taken ...*
- *I think I would prefer to be friends with ...*
- *The boy in photo 1 looks more ... than the girl in photo 2 ... because ...*

1

2

2 What does your profile photo say about you? ➜ SB (p. 11) • SF 27 (p. 70)

a) You are going to listen to an interview with a social media expert about profile photos. Read the sentences in b) first. Then guess how the sentences might continue. Write in your exercise book.

b) 02 Complete the sentences while you listen. Compare the full sentences you wrote in your exercise book with Nisha's answers. Did you manage to guess any of them correctly?

1 Profile photos have been studied in recent years because increased online communication ______________________

____

2 Nisha thinks that deciding quickly what someone is like is ______________________

____

3 If someone isn't close to the camera, it can mean they ______________________

____

4 Steve's profile photos suggest that he is ______________________

____

5 In Nisha's opinion, young people use group photos because it can ______________________

____

6 Three reasons why people might use a baby photo for their profile photo are: (1) they don't want to grow up,

(2) they think ______________________

3 Poems about identity ➜ SB (pp. 12–14)

a) Read the two poems. How do they explore the theme of identity?
Write about 100 words in your exercise book.

Poem 1 is about how someone's identity can be linked to ...

Accent

As soon as he opens his mouth, his city appears,
Written in giant neon[1] letters across his forehead[2].
His accent was made in Liverpool's melting pot[3]:
a spoonful[4] of Lancashire[5], a dollop[6] of Irish,
and a pinch[7] of Welsh –
all seasoned[8] with a sprinkle[9] of Scandinavian[10].
Down south, they hear it
And straight away they think they know him.
He must have football in his blood
(whether it's red or blue),
a spirit[11] as tough as old boots
and a cheeky[12] sense of humour.
Just for a change,
he'd love someone to ask him
who he really is.

Genetics[13]

I was born with Mom's big brown eyes.
"She's her mother's daughter," they said.
My father gave me my eyebrows[14] – two straight brush strokes[15] –
And a frown that could start World War Three.
My teeth came through crooked[16], like broken piano keys
And everybody said I had Aunt Julia's smile.
They all predicted[17]
That I would have straight, silky hair,
Dark as molasses[18], like Grandpa's. Like everyone's.
But it came through rough and curly
And dark red, like rust[19].
It's a wild beast[20] that will not be tamed[21].
But I love it.
It's the only part of me that's really mine.

b) ● Choose three short phrases from each poem that speak to your emotions.
In your exercise book, explain why you find them moving.

I think that "giant neon letters" is a good way to explain how ... "He must have football in his blood" – this is a strong image that shows how ... "like broken piano keys" – this image is good because piano keys are ... "a wild beast" – this is a funny way to describe ...

c) Share your answers to a) and b) with a partner.

d) For each poem, choose a phrase that you found difficult to understand.
What do you think it could mean? Discuss your ideas with your partner.

In the first poem, I'm not sure about the meaning of ... It could be ... What do you think?

4 Talking about imagery ➜ SB (p. 15)

a) ○ Underline the correct answer.

1 **Similes and metaphors:** cannot be combined in one image / are two common ways of creating images in the readers' minds / compare things using *as* or *like*.
2 **Metaphors:** are usually thought to be stronger than similes / are easy to recognize because they always use the verb to be / don't work in the same sentence as similes.
3 **Similes:** are always used before metaphors / often describe someone's character or appearance / suggest that one thing is another thing.

b) Go back to the poems in exercise 3. In each poem, underline at least three similes and three metaphors in different colours. Check your answers with a partner.

c) Choose one example of imagery from each poem and say why you like it/don't like it.
Share your answers with a partner.

In poem 1, I like the metaphor of the person with neon letters on his head ...
I think it's a good way to describe ...

---

[1]neon ['niːɒn] [2]forehead ['fɔːhed, 'fɒrɪd] *Stirn* [3]melting pot ['meltɪŋ pɒt] *Schmelztiegel* [4]spoonful ['spuːnfʊl] *ein Löffel* [5]Lancashire ['læŋkəʃə] *Grafschaft im Nordwesten Englands* [6]dollop ['dɒləp] *Klacks* [7]pinch [pɪnʃ] *Prise* [8]season ['siːzn] *würzen* [9]sprinkle *hier: leichter Einschlag/leichte Färbung* [10]Scandinavian [ˌskændɪ'neɪviən] [11]spirit *Geist* [12]cheeky *frech, schnippisch* [13]genetics [dʒə'netɪks] *Genetik* [14]eyebrow ['aɪbraʊ] *Augenbraue* [15]brush stroke ['brʌʃ strəʊk] *Pinselstrich* [16]crooked ['krʊkɪd] *schief* [17]predict [prɪ'dɪkt] *voraussagen* [18]molasses [məʊ'læsɪz] *Melasse, dunkelbrauner Zuckersirup* [19]rust *Rost* [20]beast [biːst] *Tier* [21]tame *zähmen*

5 Creating imagery ➔ SB (p. 15)

Look at the two photos. In your exercise book, Describe the girl and the boy (e.g. how they look, what they might be like, how they live and talk, how they might feel, what their hobbies are ...). Use metaphors and similes. Write about 100 words in your exercise book.

The girl in the first photo wants people to think she's as ...

6 ACCESS TO WORDS Describing a person's identity ➔ SB (p. 16) • Wordbank 1

a) Choose five words from the box that you might want to use in your talk in c). In your exercise book, write sentences that explain what they mean.

African-American · aggressive · ambitious · athletic · competitive · conservative · conventional · determined · emotional · famous · gay · gentle · honest · kind · liberal · musical · optimistic · original · passionate · patient · patriotic · reliable · responsible · self-confident · straight · tolerant · tough

1 A reliable person is always there when you need him/her.

2 Someone who is musical is very good at singing or playing an instrument.

b) In your exercise book, rewrite the sentences below to make the meaning stronger or weaker. Use adverbs and adjectives from the box.

(not) particularly · huge · terribly · (not) very · great · big · quite

TIP: Remember: you can search for collocations using quotation marks in a search engine. If you don't get many results, the collocation may not be very common.

1 He's the sort of person who is patient with others.

He's the sort of person who is particularly patient with others.

2 She's proud of her liberal upbringing.

3 One thing he values is adventure.

4 He's a fan of the African-American author Maya Angelou.

5 She likes volunteering.

6 She loves to read novels, but she isn't a fan of poetry.

7 They don't find indoor climbing interesting.

8 Music has always been important to him.

c) ● Prepare a two-minute talk for your class about someone you know (or a famous person or character from a book). Describe how this person sees himself/herself. Before you start, make a list of 8–10 words from a) and b) that you want to use.

7 STUDY SKILLS Improving your electronic texts ➜ SB (p. 17) • SF 15 (p. 63)

a) ○ Tick (✓) the statements that are correct.

1 Don't use more than one heading: they make a text look untidy. [✓]

2 Any photos or pictures used should fit the amount of text and the font size. [✓]

3 Empty lines between paragraphs are a waste of space. [ ]

4 It's all right to use different fonts for the captions and the body of the text. [ ]

5 Margins should be used above and below the text as well as at the sides. [✓]

6 All images must include the photographer's name. (source) [✓]

7 Standard fonts such as Arial are best. [✓]

8 Use different styles (e. g. bold and italics) to make the text visually more inviting. [✓]

b) Re-read the guidelines on p. 17 of your student's book on text layout and formatting. Note down in your exercise book the five most important things you want to remember next time you write an electronic text.

– *not too much text on page ...*

c) ● Examine the text below. Mark the parts of the text that do not follow the guidelines. You can also write keywords or short notes. Tell your partner what you would change, and why.

Hollie McNish

Hollie McNish is a British poet, writer and spoken-word performer. She was born in Reading, in southern England. Hollie first began writing poetry when she was seven but did not perform her poems on stage until she was in her twenties. Soon after that, she won several poetry competitions and became UK Slam Poetry Champion in 2009. *Hollie MCnish's poems are inspiring, powerful and written from the heart using everyday language and humour to capture her feelings. Her work is easy to understand, and she comes across as very honest. This is perhaps why up to one thousand people attend each of her live performances.* She is also very popular online, with certain videos of her reciting her poemsgoing viral and receiving milions of views. Her published books include *Papers*, **Nobody Told Me,** Cherry Pie and *Plum*. SHe has also recorded an album of poetry called Versus. Hollie McNish also co-wrote the play *Offside*, whichis about the history of women's football in the UK.

Hollie McNish has worked with other poets and spoken-word artists including Kate Tempest. She has also been involved in many poetry workshops and projects at schools. One interestingproject was at a high school, where she helped pupils to decorate their new school building with lines from poems they had written. (Photo: from the internet)

8 WORDS How to structure an opinion piece ➜ SB (p. 19)

○ Complete the text using words from the box. There are three more words than you need.

action · captions · catch · facts · fonts · headline · job · long · main · opinion · paragraph · provocative · quotes · statement · supporting · topic

Your *headline* can have different forms – a question, a ________________ or a solution – but it must ________________ the reader's attention. The ________________ of the first ________________ is to make him or her want to keep reading. Make sure it is not too ________________. Both your ________________ and opinion should be stated clearly. You can then use ________________ paragraphs to add information that backs up your ________________ statement. Do this by using ________________, statistics or other ________________ in the paragraphs. Finally, use the conclusion to remind the reader of your ________________ and suggest a solution or call for ________________.

9 REVISION Ending discrimination in sport (Simple present, simple past, modals) ➜ SB (p. 20)

a) ● Re-read section 5.1 on p. 20 of your student's book. Then read the paragraph, looking carefully at the verbs. What mistakes can you find? Underline them in the text.

Women and men now has equal status in almost all areas of professional life, so why is the pay gap still existing in sport? It simply does not makes sense. In 2017 the list of the hundred highest-paid athletes include just one woman: the tennis player Serena Williams. You know that the winners of the men's football World Cup have got $35 m in 2014, but when the US women's football team has won the women's World Cup in 2015, they got just 5.7 % of the men's pay? These is just a couple of examples of a huge gender pay gap in international sport. I am surprised that information like this do not make people angrier. Doesn't every woman has the right to receive fair pay? I am believing that the equal rights movement in sport still have a long way to go.

b) Check your answers with a partner. Then write a corrected version of the text in your exercise book.

c) Decide which of these statements express support for ending discrimination in sport. Then, in your exercise book, rewrite the other sentences so that they also express the same thing.

1 We should accept racism on the football pitch. ◯
2 International sports competitions ought to pay men and women the same. ◯
3 We absolutely must keep protesting against discrimination in sport. ◯
4 Female athletes can be expected to work for less than male athletes. ◯
5 We have to accept the idea that things will never change. ◯
6 Governments around the world should not ignore anti-racism groups. ◯
7 We ought to listen to people who support unequal pay. ◯
8 No successful athlete should earn less just because she is a woman. ◯

10 Using persuasive language ➜ SB (p. 21)

○ Underline the correct answer.

1 **Persuasion techniques:**
are words that make your reader feel angry or sad / re a useful device for improving your style and winning over your reader / suggest that your arguments are based on facts.

2 **Using rhetorical questions:**
stresses your point / makes the reader consider another point of view / shows that other people agree with you.

3 **Dramatic statistics are used to:**
get closer to your reader / underline important points / refer to events from history.

4 **Using the personal pronoun *we*:**
shows how strongly you feel / shows that everyone has the same opinion / suggests that you have something in common with your readers.

5 **Anecdotes:**
suggest that your argument is factual / show that you know the topic well / let you get closer to your reader.

11 Analysing an opinion piece ➜ SB (pp. 19–21) • SF9 (p. 60)

Look at the guidelines on pp. 19–21 of your student's book. Do you think the text below includes all the points? Write notes in your exercise book to justify your answer.

1 headline must capture reader's attention

Gendered[1] toys are dangerous!

For years, toy companies have advertised[2] cars, trucks and superhero costumes to boys, while we have been encouraged to buy dolls[3], toy kitchens and princess dresses for girls. But it is ridiculous to suggest that all children of one sex[4] like a certain kind of toy – and it is dangerous.

Gendered toys are so normal in our society that many of us do not even notice what is happening. My five-year-old cousin plays with dolls at home, but he would never tell his friends, because they think dolls are just for girls. And I know a little girl who loves cars but avoids[5] playing with them at nursery[6] because people say they are "boys' toys". Children should not have to feel ashamed[7] like this in the 21st century. Most women drive, and a father pushing his baby along in a buggy[8] is now a common sight[9]. So, we really ought not to let toy companies tell our children what they should like based on old-fashioned ideas.

When children feel that they cannot live their lives the way they want, it affects[10] their identity, and this can have a serious impact[11] on their self-confidence. The UK children's organization *ChildLine* reports that low self-esteem[12] is a growing problem: *ChildLine* provided[13] 35,244 counselling[14] sessions for children with low self-esteem in 2014–2015, and the number increased the year after. As if this were not worrying enough, gendered toys can also affect children's education, since different kinds of toys teach different skills. Therefore, experts say that children should play with the widest possible range[15] of toys. Who could argue with that?

Companies say it is traditional to separate children by sex. But did you know that until the 1970s, most toys came in bright colours such as red or yellow? A red ball could be for both boys and girls, so siblings[16] could share it. But now, toy companies can sell more if parents think their son needs a blue ball and their daughter must have a pink one.

The good news is that some parents and politicians[17] have decided to do something. There are now movements around the world that want to break down the pink/blue divide[18]. In the UK, a group called *Let Toys Be Toys* works to make toy shops stop describing products[19] as "girls' toys" and "boys' toys". In the USA, there are also groups that take the issue very seriously.

These are all positive actions, but the situation is so dangerous that I think we ought to stop buying all toys that are advertised as being just for boys or just for girls. Today the UK is the largest toy market in Europe, so if we stopped buying gendered toys, perhaps toy companies would finally start to listen.

---

[1]gendered toy [ˌdʒendəd 'tɔɪ] *Spielzeug, das durch seine Aufmachung gezielt Jungen oder Mädchen ansprechen soll*
[2]advertise sth. ['ædvətaɪz] *für etw. Werbung machen* [3]doll [dɒl] *Puppe* [4]sex [seks] *Geschlecht* [5]avoid [ə'vɔɪd] *vermeiden*
[6]nursery ['nɜːsri] *Kindergarten* [7]feel ashamed [ə'ʃeɪmd] *sich schämen* [8]buggy ['bʌgi] *Kinderwagen* [9]sight [saɪt] *Anblick*
[10]affect [ə'fekt] *sich auswirken* [11]impact ['ɪmpækt] *Einfluss* [12]low self-esteem [ləʊ ˌselfɪ'stiːm] *geringes Selbstwertgefühl*
[13]provide [prə'vaɪd] *zur Verfügung stellen* [14]counselling ['kaʊnslɪŋ] *Beratungs-* [15]range [reɪndʒ] *Spektrum*
[16]sibling ['sɪblɪŋ] *Geschwister (meist pl.)* [17]politician [ˌpɒlə'tɪʃn] *Politiker/in* [18]divide [dɪ'vaɪd] *Kluft* [19]product ['prɒdʌkt] *Produkt*

12 Work and identity ➜ SB (pp. 19–21) • SF9 (p. 60)

a) Complete the following sentence in as many ways as you can: Jobs and work can be important for people's identities because …

- … *people usually spend most of their lives working.*
- …

b) ● In your exercise book, write an opinion piece on whether jobs and work are important for people's identities. Write about 300 words. Consider the guidelines on pp. 19–21 of your student's book.

c) ● Give your text to a partner to read. Get feedback on the structure, grammar and style, e.g. headline, conclusion, use of tenses, persuasion techniques.

d) ● Think of improvements you could make. Then edit your text and read it.

13 On the news (The passive: present progressive form) ➜ SB (p. 23)

a) A radio journalist is reporting from a science and technology fair. Complete her sentences using the present progressive passive.

1 All the different projects *are being set up* (set up).

2 Visitors ______ (give) a plan of the fair as they arrive.

3 An amazing new kind of engine ______ (present) at this stand.

4 We ______ (take) to meet last year's winner.

5 I have a tiny camera here and I ______ (show) how to use it.

6 Lots of new devices ______ (test) at the fair today.

7 How exciting – the winners ______ (announced) right now on the stage!

8 I ______ (lead) backstage now to interview Celia McBride, who has won first prize.

b) A reporter is talking about an escaped snake on the radio. Complete his sentences in the present progressive. Use the passive form if needed.

1 A dangerous snake *is being hunted* (hunt) after it escaped from its owner's house today.

2 Students ______ (prevent) from entering the college next door.

3 Police officers ______ (plan) to search the college in the next hour.

4 Neighbours ______ (tell) to call the police if they see the snake.

5 A search of the local park ______ (plan) for this afternoon.

6 Jill Brown ______ (hope) that her pet hasn't gone far.

14 Protecting your information online ➜ SB (p. 23) • SF 22–24 (p. 68)

a) ● 03 You will hear a German radio report about teens and online security.
Before listening, explain these German words in English in your exercise book:

Identitätsmissbrauch | Privatsphäre | Sachschaden | Strafanzeige

Then listen. Take notes on the dangers of posting party invitations online.

b) ● You are chatting online with Connor, your school's Canadian exchange student. He is planning a party when his German host family is away. He tells you he wants to post about it on social media. Tell him in English about the report you heard and what could happen if he posted the family's address online. Write about 100 words in your exercise book.

Connor, I really don't think you should ...

15 The meaning behind the flags ➜ SB (p. 24) • SF 31 (pp. 71–72)

a) ● In your exercise book, describe the photos. Write about 30 words about each one.

Photo 1 shows an athlete ...

b) ● What are the reasons for using the flags in each photo?
In your exercise book, write three to four sentences for each picture.

In photo 1 it looks as if ...
The flags are there because they express/stand for ...

16 The Union Jack ➜ SB (p. 24) • SF 27 (p. 70)

a) ○ 04 What is the report about? Listen once. Then (circle) A, B or C.

- **A** the history of the Union Jack
- **B** why the Union Jack became a fashion symbol
- **C** problems that musicians, designers and companies had with the Union Jack

b) 04 Listen again and complete the sentences.

1 In the 1960s London became a center of fashion. ✓

2 The Union Jack causes bad memories for some people because it was used by politicians groups ✓

3 After the 1960s the music industry used the Union Jack as a cover for their albums/Highlight identity

4 In its adverts the energy company uses a green version of union jack. ✓

5 The presenter doesn't agree that the UK is still cool.

6 The Union Jack's design is recognized abroad because it's also used by other countrys ✓

7 The main reason why the Union Jack is so popular is that it is fantastic image for designers ✓

8 Designers don't need permission to use the flag because the design isn't protected ✓

17 EXTRA BACKGROUND FILE Tech identity ➜ SB (p. 26) • SF 1 (p. 56)

a) Read the questions below. Then go to p. 26 of your student's book and scan the four texts. Write short answers to the questions.

1 Name two things a DNA test can prove. If you are involved into crime who are your siblings, If ~~if~~ you are father...

2 What is some people's opinion of DeepFace? They ~~fel~~ feel stalked

3 What information about your sleep do fitness trackers record? How long and well you sleep.

4 Name three things that might happen to your medical data. It could send to huge companies/They might get stolen/load up to online platform

5 What happens when you use a smartcard on the train? It's easily to find out where you are

6 What do the wi-fi sensors use to record your movements? They connect with your Smartphone

b) ● In your exercise book, summarize how new technology can be used to collect data about people and why the data is not always safe. Use your answers from a) and other information from p. 26 of your student's book. Write about 180 words.

Today there are new technologies that can ...

18 WORDS Poetry slams ➜ SB (p. 26)

Complete the sentences with words from the box in the correct form.

appeal to · consider · emphatic · expressive · focus on · gender · identity · importance · metaphor · original · passionate · perspective · poet · receive · simile · unlike

A poetry slam is a competition in which (1) poets read their (2) ______ work in front of an audience. The first poetry slams were held in Chicago in the 1980s. Slam poetry uses many of the traditional devices found in poetry, such as (3) ______ and (4) ______. But, (5) ______ traditional poetry, slam poetry (6) ______ using a person's (7) ______ to protest about social problems of great (8) ______, such as discrimination based on race or (9) ______. It is interesting to learn about these issues from different (10) ______, and that is one of the reasons why poetry slams (11) ______ so many people. The performers are very (12) ______ about their message. They use an (13) ______ style to catch the audience's attention and (14) ______ language to connect with them. The performers (15) ______ points from the audience. Slam poetry is still quite new, but it is already (16) ______ an art form.

19 LISTENING COURSE Connected speech ➜ SB (p. 27) • SF 27 (p. 70)

a) 05 Read the sentences. Listen to how they are spoken in normal speech, then draw lines to link the words that are connected. Listen again and check.

1 Where‿is‿he? He should‿have‿been‿here by now!
2 I don't think there are any cakes left – sorry!
3 Tell her she'll have to wait. There's a big queue.
4 He's as old as her brother, but he looks younger.
5 Try and have a nice time – if you can.
6 I hope her dog's OK. He doesn't look well, does he?

b) 06 Read the sentences. Then listen to the sentences spoken at normal speed and write down the missing words. Listen again and check.

1 Will he be going to your aunt's party?
2 How many times ______ London?
3 I sent ______ weeks ago.
4 ______ coming too?
5 ______ late again?
6 ______ this bottle, would you?

1 WORDS A profile

Complete the text with correct words, especially adverbs and adjectives as modifiers.

My grandma Lin is the sort of person who r*eally* (1) likes to be around people. Her family is a **h**________ (2) part of her life: she **a**________ (3) loves visiting her children. She has always been a **f**________ (4) hard-working person. She didn't have a **p**________ (5) **c**________ (6) career as a young woman: she was one of the first computer programmers at a large bank. She is **q**________ (7) proud of what she achieved there. One person who **i**________ (8) her was her father. He had his own company and was **e**________ (9) hard-working. Maybe that's why she has always been so **a**________ (10) and focused on success. One thing Grandma Lin values a **l**________ (11) is music. She has always been **v**________ (12) **p**________ (13) about it and she is a **g**________ (14) fan of the opera. I don't think she is very **m**________ (15) herself, though: she says she's **n**________ (16) **e**________ (17) good at singing.

2 Why is he being photographed? (The passive: present progressive form)

You are watching a film with your American host family, but you don't understand everything. Write questions in the present progressive passive in your exercise book.

1 man/photograph/why/that
Why is that man being photographed?
2 arrest/scientists/why
3 car/her/stop/why
4 take/where/device
5 watch/that/why/woman
6 information/send/how

3 Writing an opinion piece: language structures (Simple present, simple past, modals)

a) Read the statements about how to use different tenses in an opinion piece. Tick (✓) the statements that are correct.

1 For general statements, the simple present is often used. ◯
2 When you give examples from your experience, you should only use the simple past. ◯
3 You can use the simple present to support your argument with examples from research. ◯

b) Kyle believes that technology that identifies us is very scary. He thinks that people should do something about the issue, so he has written an opinion piece. Underline the correct modal verb.

1 We **mustn't/might/could** let companies have access to our personal information.
2 People **can't/ought to/may** learn to protect their smartphones.
3 We **needn't/should/can't** realize that we pay for 'free' services with our private information.
4 The problem is that some programs **should/can/ought to** identify us in the street – that is creepy.
5 Nobody **have to/needn't/has to** accept this, though – we have a choice.
6 I think people **need/shouldn't/must** wake up and realize that it's time to change things.

4 Writing an opinion piece: tips for Maddison

Your Australian friend Maddison wants to write an opinion piece for her school magazine.
She has never written one before. Write her an email with a list of tips.
Give advice on structure and style. Write about eight tips.

Hi Maddison! Here are the tips I wanted to send you.

- *Use a headline that catches the reader's attention.*
- *You should ...*
- *...*

Let me read it when you've finished!

5 Money and identity: writing an opinion piece

a) Consider why money can be important for people's identities.
In your exercise book, express your view in a few sentences, e. g.

Rich people have a responsibility to help the world's poor.
And being generous makes us happier too.

Advertisements try to make us buy things to become a certain kind of person.
But we are more than what we own.

b) Write an opinion piece about money and identity on your computer.
Write about 300 words. Consider your tips from exercise 4.

Check: Writing

a) Vergleiche deine Antworten mit den Lösungen auf Seite 79 im Workbook.
b) Schätze deine Antworten mit einem grünen oder roten Gesicht ein.

	☺	☹	
1 Hast du in Aufgabe 1 Vokabeln gewusst, die dir helfen, über Identität zu sprechen und ein Profil zu schreiben?	○	○	→ 1
2 Hast du in Aufgabe 2 das Passiv des *present progressive* richtig eingesetzt?	○	○	→ 2
3 Hast du in Aufgabe 3 gewusst, wie man in einem *opinion piece* die Zeitformen und Modalverben richtig verwendet?	○	○	→ 3
4 Hast du in Aufgabe 4 und Aufgabe 5 gewusst, wie man ein *opinion piece* mit korrekter Struktur und im richtigen Stil schreibt?	○	○	→ 4

c) Wenn du dich rot eingeschätzt hast, schau dir die rechte Spalte an.
Die Nummern führen dich zu den passenden Übungen im Skills Training (S. 14–15).
Dort kannst du gezielt Writing trainieren.

1 WORDS Writing a profile

a) Find the missing adjectives from this unit.

1 A person who is ______________________ about poetry really loves poems.

2 Someone who is good at all sports is very ______________________.

3 Some dogs are gentle, and others are quite ______________________.

4 If you like to do things the same way as everyone else, you're ______________________.

5 She comes from a very ______________________ family: they all play instruments.

6 We don't know much about him: he's quite ______________________.

7 Her parents are often open to new ideas: they're quite ______________________.

8 I've read books like that before. The story isn't very ______________________.

b) Underline the correct modifier in each sentence.

1 Tom is a **really/huge/fairly** fan of American football.

2 My upbringing was not **fairly/particularly/not a lot** conventional.

3 Technology isn't a **really/bit/big** part of her life.

4 One thing I value **a lot/really/quite** is time with my family.

5 My friends think I'm **great/quite/a lot** reliable.

6 Their dialect isn't **absolutely/very/not particularly** easy to understand.

c) In your exercise book, write a profile of a friend or member of your family. Use adverbs and adjectives as modifiers. Write about 150 words.

2 A football match (The passive: present progressive form)

A journalist is reporting from a women's World Cup match. Complete his sentences using the present progressive passive.

1 This match ______________________ (watch) by millions around the world.

2 Today you ______________________ (show) the very best of women's football!

3 The Swedish goalkeeper ______________________ (test) today.

4 The teams ______________________ (lead) onto the pitch for the second half.

5 The USA's best player ______________________ (give) a red card.

6 The winners ______________________ (interview) by the international media.

7 A trophy ______________________ (bring) onto the pitch.

8 The winners ______________________ (photograph) by thousands of fans.

3 Animal rights (Simple present, simple past, modals)

a) Read the paragraph, looking carefully at the verb tenses. In your exercise book, correct the mistakes you find.

People are sometimes asking whether animals ought to has more rights. I believe they should. Sadly, it is a fact that cruel treatment of animals is something that happen in every country around the world, in zoos, homes and the fashion industry, among others. On average, every 30 seconds someone in England and Wales is calling the RSPCA – the UK's organization for protecting animals. In 2007, the Animal Welfare Act has became law in England, but the problem is still existing. In 2016 the RSPCA has received over one million phone calls about animals that have needed help. In the same year, it rescued almost 130,000 animals. Many people are thinking that the law still does not protect animals enough.

b) Look carefully at the modals in the sentences below. In your exercise book, rewrite the sentences so that they express support for animal rights.

1 Companies that test make-up on animals needn't pay a fine.

2 We might ignore the fact that many zoo animals live in terrible conditions.

3 People can stop protesting against the cruel treatment of animals.

4 Some industries do not consider animal rights important, but we may accept this.

4 Work and identity: editing your text → *SF 9 (p. 60)*

You are going to edit the opinion piece that you wrote for exercise 5b) on p. 13.

a) Re-read your text. Does it include everything from the checklist below? Tick (✓) every step that you have completed.

1 Have you written an interesting headline that catches the reader's attention?	○
2 Is the first paragraph short?	○
3 Have you stated your opinion and topic clearly in the first paragraph?	○
4 Have you backed up your main statement with	
– statistics	○
– historical facts	○
– quotes	○
– anecdotes?	○
5 Have you included the personal pronouns *I*, *you* or *we*?	○
6 Have you used expressive language?	○
7 Does your text contain at least one rhetorical question?	○
8 Are the verbs used correctly?	○
9 Do the modals express what you want them to express?	○
10 Does your conclusion restate your opinion and then offer a solution/call to action?	○

b) Edit your text so that all the steps in the checklist are complete, then read your text again.

2 Unit

What makes a community?

1

1 Technology and community ➔ *SB (pp. 30–31) • SF 31 (pp. 71–72)*

a) ○ Look at the photos.
- Describe the setting, the people and what they are doing.
- Why do you think they have come together?
- How might these activities make them feel part of a community?

Write in your exercise book.

1

2

3

4

Picture 1 shows a group of people talking … They seem to be in a … I think they have come together to …
This activity might make them feel part of a community because …

b) Look at the following pairs of activities. Choose one pair and explain which activity you would prefer to do, and why. Consider aspects such as fun, costs, time, etc. Write about 100–150 words in your exercise book.

1 staying in touch with your friends via social media – meeting your friends to chat and play games

Staying in touch with friends via social media is easy because …
But I also think it's easier to concentrate on what someone is saying if you are …
I would prefer to meet my friends to chat and play games because …

2 supporting a foreign football team and watching their matches on TV or online – supporting a local football team and going to their matches

3 doing yoga at home with online videos – going to a yoga class near your home

4 buying most things you need online – buying most things from the local shops

c) ● Comment on this statement. Justify your answer.
Write about 150–200 words in your exercise book.

"Technology is destroying our feeling of community."

2 A meeting of two Americas: beliefs and opinions ➔ SB (pp. 32–35) • SF 2, 5 (pp. 56, 58)

a) Joanna says about the American missionaries, "Their beliefs are not my beliefs" (l. 183).
Re-read parts 3 and 4 of the text on pp. 33–35 of your student's book. Then list three things that the missionaries believe that are different from what Joanna believes at this point in the novel. You can use the words in the box to help you.

children · food · share · take care · things · visit

What the missionaries believe:	What Joanna believes:
1 It is not clear whether the Isabo women ________	1 It is clear that the Isabo women ________
2 You need to bring ________	2 You don't need ________
3 It isn't important to ________	3 You should ________

b) Re-read lines 243–281 on p. 35 of your student's book. In your exercise book, explain the Isabo people's opinion about the missionaries in this part of the text. How do the Isabo react to the missionaries? Write about 100 words.

The Isabo people are surprised when the missionaries tell them to "make pui" in ...

c) ● Assess how useful the American missionaries' work is, as far as you can tell from what you have read so far. Write about 50–100 words in your exercise book.

In my opinion, the American missionaries' work is ...

3 A phone call from South America (Indirect speech) ➔ SB (p. 36)

Brandon from California is staying in a village in Peru as part of a volunteering project. On a trip to a nearby city, he phones his brother, Sam. Read these lines from their conversation. Then imagine you are Sam. A few days later, you tell your grandmother what Brandon said. Write in your exercise book.

1 Are the people in the village friendly? — The villagers are really friendly. — I feel part of the community already.

2 Where are you staying? — I'm staying with a family, in their house. — It's great!

3 How is your project going? — It's coming along really well. — Everyone thinks the community center will make a big difference.

4 Do you like the food? — I find it a little boring. — But it's healthy, at least.

5 When will you call again? — I don't know. — It'll probably be next month.

6 Will you visit any other countries before coming home? — No, I probably won't. — I'm going to travel to a few different cities, though.

1 *I asked Brandon / I wanted to know whether the people in the village were friendly. He said they were really friendly. He added that he felt part of the community already.*

4 Getting to know the volunteers (Indirect speech: *advise, promise, suggest, …*) ➜ *SB (p. 36)*

Use a verb from the box to report what the other volunteers said to Brandon. Use each verb only once. Write in your exercise book.

advise · *invite* · offer · promise · refuse · suggest · tell · ask

1 **Liz:** "Come and eat with us, Brandon!"

Liz invited Brandon to eat with them.

2 **Tim:** "If you like, you can borrow my camera."

3 **Liz:** "Why don't we go swimming in the afternoon?"

4 **Carlos:** "I'll show you the school."

5 **Carlos:** "Rosa's grandfather lives there."

6 **Tim:** "If I were you, I'd just eat with your fingers."

7 **Liz:** "Do you miss your friends?"

8 **Carlos:** "I'm not eating your candy – yuck!"

5 Appropriate behaviour: out and about in England ➜ *SB (p. 37) • Wordbank 2*

a) ○ 07 Listen to the three conversations. Which situations are they talking about? Write the number of the conversation in the box.

☐ talking to people on the train
☐ making phone calls in public places
☐ staying safe as a pedestrian
☐ getting on the bus

b) 07 Listen again and complete the following sentences:

1 **Conv. 1:** The woman was angry because ______________________

2 **Conv. 1:** Liam thinks queueing is ______________________

3 **Conv. 2:** Max was uncomfortable because ______________________

4 **Conv. 2:** Max's solution to the problem was to ______________________

5 **Conv. 2:** Liam thinks Max's behaviour was ______________________

6 **Conv. 3:** Liam thinks Max's way of crossing the road is ______________________

6 Appropriate behaviour: what was the problem? ➜ *SB (p. 37) • SF 4–5 (pp. 57–58) • Wordbank 2*

Alice from Scotland is an exchange student at your school. Read the paragraphs from an email she has sent you. In your exercise book, write a reply to each paragraph in English. Explain each problem and tell Alice what she should do next time. Write about 50 words for each situation.

1 I was on the tram on Friday evening and two women shouted "Hallo, hallo!" at me. I didn't know them, so I didn't say hello back! When I got off, I realized I'd forgotten my big yellow scarf. They must have seen it. So why didn't they tell me?

2 We were in a big shopping centre on Saturday and I went to the toilet. There was a woman near the door with a plate full of coins. When I walked past her on the way out, she shouted at me. Why?

3 I asked Lucas's mum if we could go back to the shopping centre on Sunday to look at clothes. She said no! I guess she thinks clothes shopping is boring or a waste of time. I was really disappointed …

4 I know how important it is to throw your rubbish in the right bin here, so I put my plastic bottle and my magazine in the yellow bin outside Lucas's flat. Then a neighbour said, "So was macht man nicht!" Why? That's how we do it at home …

1 *The problem was that the people on the tram were … But you didn't … If it happens again, you should …*

7 LISTENING COURSE Different accents ➔ SB (p. 39) • SF 27 (p. 70)

a) ○ Think about the standard British and American English accents. Which accent has:

1 a weak **t**? ______________________
3 a strong **t**? ______________________
2 a weak **r**? ______________________
4 a strong **r**? ______________________

b) 08 Say the sentences as you think they would be in BE and AE, paying attention to the **r**s and **t**s. Record yourself. Then listen and check.

1 I'll buy a computer later.
2 I always drink cold water.
3 Does his daughter have a car?
4 The park there is much nicer.

8 LISTENING COURSE Standard BE and AE ➔ SB (p. 39) • SF 27 (p. 70)

a) ○ 09 You will hear six pairs of sentences. One speaker is British and the other is American. In each pair, one word is the same. Write it down.

1 ______________ 3 ______________ 5 ______________
2 ______________ 4 ______________ 6 ______________

b) 09 Listen again and repeat the sentences. Record yourself. Then listen and check.

c) 10 Say the words below as you think they would be pronounced in BE and AE. Listen and check.

lot – plant – enthusiastic – problem – plaster – obvious – mask – job – knew – basket

9 LISTENING COURSE Different British accents ➔ SB (p. 39) • SF 27 (p. 70)

a) ● 11 How might these words be pronounced in the following regional accents? Say each word in standard British pronunciation, then in the regional accent. Record yourself. Then listen and check.

1 bright (Scotland)
3 bath (England: north)
5 mouse (Northern Ireland)
2 scarf (England: west)
4 coat (Scotland)
6 shout (London/southeast)

b) 12 You will hear three university students talking about a community gardening project in London. Listen to their accents. Where are they from? Circle A, B or C.

A northern England, London, Scotland
B London, Northern Ireland, northern England
C Scotland, Northern Ireland, northern England

c) 12 Listen again. What are three advantages of having trees in the city?

____
____
____
____

10 While watching the plane land, … (Participle clauses with *after, before, since,* …) ➜ *SB (p. 42)*

○ Make one sentence out of two. Use participle clauses with the conjunction given. Write in your exercise book.

1 Alicia watches the plane land. She talks to Joanna. (while)

While watching the plane land, Alicia talks to Joanna.

2 The missionaries get out of their plane. Then they take boxes of stuff into Angel's house. (after)

3 Joanna talks to the old man. She gets angry. (while)

4 Brandon arrived in Peru in July. He has learned a lot about the country. (since)

5 Sam called his grandmother. Then he played a computer game. (after)

6 Liz left the project. She organized a party in the village. (before)

11 Wanting to visit the missionaries, … (Participle clauses meaning *because* …) ➜ *SB (p. 42)*

a) ○ Match the main clauses on the left to a reason on the right.

1 Alicia goes to Angel's house because
2 Joanna is almost drooling because
3 Margarita gives away her chocolate because
4 Alicia just nods at Joanna because
5 The missionaries have brought lots of stuff because
6 The villagers don't laugh out loud because

she is very hungry.
she wants to share.
they don't want to insult the visitors.
they think it is necessary to do so.
she wants to visit the missionaries.
she doesn't know what to say.

b) Rewrite the sentences you formed in a), using a participle clause (-ing …/Not -ing …) at the beginning of the sentence. Write in your exercise book.

1 *Wanting to visit the missionaries, Alicia goes to Angel's house.*

12 California Volunteers (Participle clauses meaning *and* …) ➜ *SB (p. 42)*

○ Using participle clauses, rewrite each sentence in two different ways.
Write in your exercise book.

1 Our volunteers travel to different countries and offer support to local communities.

Our volunteers travel to different countries, offering support to local communities.
Travelling to different countries, our volunteers offer support to local communities.

2 The organization's volunteers live in villages and spend a lot of time with the locals.

3 Many of the young people try out new activities and develop new skills.

4 Brandon worked in Peru for six months and helped to build a community centre.

5 Stacey visits schools in California and advises students who are interested in volunteering.

6 Barbara works in a big office and supports the organization's director.

13 A book review: *The Help* → SB (pp. 41–43) • SF 1, 12 (pp. 56, 62)

a) Skim the review. What is the novel about? Circle the correct answer.

A African-Americans who work on farms in the 1960s and experience racism

B a young woman who writes a book about African-American women working for white families

C a group of young girls in Jackson, Mississippi, who support the civil rights movement

The Help

The Help is a 2009 historical novel by the American author Kathryn Stockett. It is set in Jackson, Mississippi, in 1962, and has three main narrators. 22-year-old Skeeter has just returned home from college with dreams of becoming a writer. But, after arriving at her family's cotton farm, she is surprised to find that her beloved maid Constantine – the woman who looked after her during her childhood – is gone, and nobody seems to know what happened to her. Aibileen is an African-American maid in her 50s who has recently lost her son in an accident at work. She works for rich white people, looking after their children and their homes. She is currently caring for her seventeenth white child, Mae Mobley. Minny is Aibileen's friend and is also a maid. She keeps losing job after job because she is rude to people, but she manages to get a position working for a woman who has just moved to the town.

With great warmth and sensitivity, the author tells the story of how these three women try to change their town and their community. As the civil rights movement develops, Skeeter realizes that many of the African-American maids are being treated unfairly by their white employers. She decides to write a book about their experiences, reporting what is happening. She wants to interview local maids, and at first none of them trust her, but Aibileen and Minny later agree to talk to her, eventually getting more maids to agree as well. But will the book endanger their jobs and their safety? What will Skeeter's privileged friends and family think of her when the book is published? And will she ever find out what happened to Constantine?

Skeeter's book mirrors the novel itself, telling stories of cruel treatment and racism by the white families of Jackson – but also tales of kindness and love, since some of the maids' experiences are positive. Although the main themes of racial segregation, racism, politics and social change dominate the novel, there are also some less serious moments that make the reader laugh out loud. The characters are interesting and varied and, by writing about events from history, Stockett makes the plot feel very real. It seems that Stockett, who was born and raised in Jackson herself and worked in the publishing industry just like Skeeter before writing her novel, has based at least some of the story on her own experiences.

This is a moving and enjoyable account of life in early 1960s Mississippi, told through the eyes of a group of people who were often treated as though they were invisible. I would recommend this highly readable novel to anyone who is interested in 20th-century history – especially the human stories behind historical events.

b) Read the review in detail and complete the sentences with information from the text. Write in your exercise book.

1 Returning to the farm, Skeeter does not expect to find that …

2 Aibileen has looked after …

3 At first, no maids want to be interviewed because …

4 Skeeter's book shows that not all of the maids …

5 The story seems real because it …

6 The author probably got some ideas for the plot from …

c) Look at the guidelines for writing book reviews on pp. 41–43 of your student's book. Do you think this writer has followed all the guidelines? Write about 100 words in your exercise book explaining what you would improve.

d) Would you like to read the book? Say why (not). Write about 100 words in your exercise book.

TIP: When explaining whether you would like to read a novel, you can mention aspects such as:
- the plot
- the themes
- the setting
- the characters
- how the book makes the reader feel
- what the reader can learn from the book

14 The repair café project ➔ SB (p. 45) • SF 22–24 (p. 68)

You are part of a 'repair café' project and want to post information about it on an international youth-in-action website. Read the text below and write a short description in English for the website. Write complete sentences. Write about 80–100 words in your exercise book.

Unser im Januar 2016 gegründetes Repair-Café – eines von 300 in Deutschland – erfreut sich großer Beliebtheit. Zu jeder Veranstaltung empfangen wir ca. 40 Besucher. Wir und die rund 1500 Repair-Cafés weltweit verfolgen ein Ziel, nämlich unnötigen Müll zu vermeiden und somit der Wegwerfkultur den Kampf anzusagen. Auf diesem Wege bringen wir Menschen zusammen, die sich für die Umwelt engagieren wollen. Darüber hinaus besteht die Möglichkeit, handwerkliche Fähigkeiten zu erlernen, denn zahlreiche Freiwillige bieten anderen ihre Hilfe an, nicht mehr funktionsfähige Alltags- und Gebrauchsgegenstände zu reparieren. So haben wir bereits einige Wasserkocher, Fahrräder, Staubsauger, Lampen oder auch Kleidung und Spielzeug in Ordnung gebracht. Gelegentlich setzen wir sogar 3D-Drucker ein, um zerbrochene und nicht mehr verfügbare Bauteile herzustellen.

Starthilfe erhielten wir von einer in den Niederlanden ansässigen Organisation, die ein Netzwerk für alle, die ein eigenes Repair-Café gründen wollen, koordiniert. Die Idee des Repair-Café stammt auch aus den Niederlanden, wo 2009 das erste Repair-Café gegründet wurde.

Our repair café was started in January 2016 ...

15 She does not want to join the project (Forms of emphasis) ➔ SB (p. 46) • SF 27 (p. 70)

a) 13 There should only be one emphatic do/did in each sentence. Decide which verb the speaker wants to emphasize and underline it.

1 I think she **wants/does want** to join the project, no matter what she **says /does say**.

2 Shelley doesn't remember whether she **closed /did close** the office windows. She **closed/did close** them: I saw her do it.

3 However hard it **seems/does seem**, we **need/do need** to use our cars less often to save the planet.

4 Please **call/do call** the volunteer manager if you have any problems after you **arrive /do arrive**.

b) 14 In your exercise book, rewrite the sentences in this way: It's .../It was ... + relative clause.

1 Joanna wore the ring, not Margarita.

It was Joanna who wore the ring, not Margarita.

2 Nimeran didn't bring a bird; he brought a leg of deer.

3 Alicia went in a plane, not a helicopter.

4 Nimeran didn't speak Spanish; Angel did.

c) 15 In your exercise book, rewrite the sentences. Complete them with the correct -self/-selves pronoun.

1 Alicia wants to try it ____.

2 Angel tried to carry all the boxes ____, but he couldn't.

3 Why don't we try doing it ____?

4 Before I give her a piece of chocolate, I'll try a bit ____.

d) 16 In your exercise book, rewrite the sentences using two of the three adverbs.

1 The snakes are dangerous in this region; we need to keep them away from the village. (really/extremely/such)

The snakes are extremely dangerous in this region; we really need to keep them away from the village.

2 It was an amazing project – I'm pleased I took part. (completely/so/absolutely)

3 I forgot to phone my parents. They'll be angry. (such/so/completely)

4 You shouldn't waste your time reading that. It's a silly book. (such/never/really)

e) Read out your sentences from a), b), c) and d) with the correct intonation. Record yourself. Then listen and check.

16 Ideas for saving water (The gerund after prepositions) ➔ *SB (p. 46)*

Complete these sentences from a website about saving water.
Use the correct preposition and the gerund of a verb in the box.

follow · save (2 x) · take · turn · use

1 We have plenty of ideas *for saving* water at home.

2 Many people are now deciding ________________ baths: showers are better.

3 Have you ever thought ________________ water from the shower again, to wash your car?

4 ________________ off the tap when cleaning your teeth, you can save six litres per minute.

5 There are many advantages ________________ water.

6 One good reason ________________ these steps: you'll pay less for your water.

17 ACCESS TO WORDS Taking a stand ➔ *SB (p. 47)*

You are going to prepare words to help you present an issue on which you think more people should take a stand. Then you will give a one-minute talk about the issue.

a) Choose five nouns from the box. In your exercise book, write sentences to explain what each word means.

activist · campaign · citizen · conference · democracy · diversity · initiative · involvement · MP · opinion poll · petition · policy · politician · pressure group · referendum · safety · signature

1 *An activist is a person who fights for something that he/she believes in.*

b) Find a partner. Don't tell each other which words you chose from the box in a).
Read out your sentences from a) without the words from the box. Guess each other's words.

c) Complete the sentences with a suitable verb in the correct form.
Write the sentences with the verb and noun collocations in your exercise book.
Compare your answers.

1 In 2016 the UK ____ a referendum on leaving the EU.

2 Some people ____ activists who were trying to persuade the public to vote.

3 Many citizens believed that a referendum was a good way to ____ democracy.

4 When the 'Leave' campaign won, thousands ____ demonstrations organized around the UK.

5 People also ____ petitions to demand a second referendum, because the result was so close.

d) ● Read the paragraph. Some of the prepositions are wrong.
In your exercise book, correct the mistakes you find.

I believe that everyone must take a stand in the pollution of our oceans. Environmental organizations report that a lorryload of rubbish is thrown into the sea every minute. Organizations such as Greenpeace campaign about this disgusting activity, but we can all help. There is a lot we can do: come together and demonstrate over marine pollution, take part on marches, sign petitions, campaign against stricter laws and give money for groups that protest around pollution.

e) ● Prepare a one-minute talk for your class about an issue on which you think more people should take a stand (e. g. problems faced by homeless people or experiments on animals).
Explain how you think people should get involved.
Before you start, make a list of 8–10 words or phrases from a), c) and d) that you want to use.

18 EXTRA Politics in the UK and the US ➔ SB (pp. 48–49) • SF 3–6 (pp. 56–58)

a) Underline the correct answers. You will find all the information you need on pp. 48–49 of your student's book.

The head of state is not elected in the UK, but the majority of British people are happy to **let the Queen appoint him or her/keep the monarchy/just elect the house of Lords**. The rules for voting depend on where you live. For example, you have to be 18 to vote in most parts of the UK, but **Scottish/Welsh/Northern Irish** people can vote at 16. Three out of four countries in the UK can vote for regional parliaments: the only one that cannot is **Northern Ireland/England/Wales**. Referendums are held **if enough voters want them/ in Scotland only/on important topics only**.

In the USA, around **a quarter/a third/a fifth** of people are registered as a member of one of the big parties. This is often a requirement for **voting in a referendum/voting in the primaries/joining a pressure group**. The Republicans and the Democrats are the only US parties that **still exist today/hold seats in the House of Commons/really have a chance at federal level**. Party members can try to get elected, but they must be **25/30/39** before they can be elected to the Senate.

b) Naomi is 17 and Scottish. Lachlan is 18 and comes from the USA. Read the statements about their rights to vote and to get involved in politics. Tick (✓) the statements that are true. Write corrected versions of the false statements in your exercise book.

1 Being under 18, Naomi can't vote in any elections yet. ◯
2 Naomi is already old enough to join a party. ◯
3 Once Naomi is 18, she will have the right to stand for election to the House of Lords. ◯
4 Naomi can't vote for a head of state, but Lachlan can help to choose the next president. ◯
5 Naomi can't vote in an initiative because they don't exist in Scotland. ◯
6 Since Lachlan is already 18, he can vote in local, state and federal elections. ◯
7 If Lachlan joins a party, he can try to get elected to the House of Representatives. ◯
8 Lachlan will have to wait until he is 25 before he can organize an initiative at federal level. ◯

c) ● Imagine you became a member of the *Bundestag*. What one thing would you do to make life better for young people? How/why would you do it? What would the advantages be for your local community? Write about 200 words in your exercise book.

If I were a member of the Bundestag, the one thing I would do to help young people would be to make/create/give ...

19 WORDS A profile of a young MP ➔ SB (pp. 48–49) • Wordbank 3

avoid · campaign · capital · dynamic · elect · emphasize · involvement · meeting · MP · party · policy · political · politician · referendum · stand

○ Complete the sentences with words from the box in the correct form.

Mhairi Black was *elected* to the UK's House of Commons in 2015 aged 20 years and 237 days, making her the youngest __________, or 'Baby of the House'. She was still a student at the University of Glasgow at the time. But her __________ career actually started a few years earlier. She joined a __________ – the SNP – in 2011, before a __________ was held on Scotland becoming an independent country. She says her ________________ in the 'Yes' ______________ made her interested in becoming a ______________ . In her first speech in parliament, Black took a ___________ against the government's _____________ on unemployment and social issues, ________________ how unfair they were. The video went viral. Black is passionate and _____________ and she never ____________ saying what she thinks. When she isn't in the UK's ____________ for ______________ at parliament, she lives in Scotland.

20 STUDY SKILLS Adam's slides ➜ SB (p. 50)

a) ○ You are at an international youth conference. Adam from Wales is giving a short presentation later today. He is nervous because he will be using a large screen on stage for the first time. He emails you his slides and asks you to help him improve them. Look at his slides.

1

International Youth Conference
24–27 May, Germany
How young people
can get involved in politics
so that they can help to
make the world a better place
By Adam Griffiths

2

Who am I?
My name is Adam Griffiths. I come from Newport, which is a city close to Cardiff in Wales, and I have been a member of Welsh Labour (a large political party) since I was 16, because I'm passionate about politics, and I think that the media reports that say that young people are not interested in politics are NOT TRUE.

3

Why don't young people get involved in politics?
They think: I'm too young, nobody will listen to me, I don't know enough about politics/how the world works, politics is boring, politicians are all bad people, etc.

None of this is true!

4

Why young people MUST get involved in politics:
- We can't expect things to change if we don't do anything. And by the way, complaining about the government isn't taking action!
- The world is changing – we must change too.
- We have opinions about the world we live in, and we need to make our voices heard.
- We can make our countries' parliaments more diverse and open to modern ideas.

We can start by:
- voting!
- thinking about what causes we care about!
- going to local meetings and speaking!

5

It's time for young people like us to make our voices heard in politics.

6

Any questions?

b) Re-read the guidelines for making slides on p. 95 and p. 97 of your student's book. How could Adam improve his slides? Write keywords. Then rewrite Adam's presentation on a computer. With a partner, talk about the revised version.

1 We do need to take action (Emphatic *do* and other forms of emphasis)

Rewrite each sentence four times, adding emphasis in a different way each time.

1 Young people need to start campaigning.

2 My MP gets involved in local projects.

2 *Boxes of Hope:* a community project (Gerund after prepositions)

be · bring · do · feel · give · make · receive · start

Complete the text with the correct preposition and the gerund of a verb in the box.

Boxes of Hope Cardiff is a community project that was set up by Bev Jones in 2017. She was tired (1) ________________ sad about children in Cardiff whose parents didn't have any money for Christmas presents, and she had the idea (2) ________________ something to help. Bev told her friends that she was thinking (3) ________________ her own initiative, and many of them were interested (4) ________________ part of it. They bought presents that they thought young children would be keen (5) ________________ – mainly toys, books and sweets. The gifts were packed into boxes and given to parents as a way (6) ________________ sure that they had something to give their children on Christmas Day. "I believe (7) ________________ the gift of hope at Christmas," explains Bev, who works on the project all year round. She says she dreams (8) ________________ the initiative to all regions of Wales in the future.

3 The European Parliament in Brussels

a) Your class is planning a trip to Belgium. You are looking for information about visiting the European Parliament in Brussels. You find these pages on English-language websites. Skim the three texts. Mark the text in which you might find the information you need.

b) Scan the texts to find the answers to these two questions (underline the parts):

1 How can you watch the European Parliament's public meetings?
2 Do you need to buy tickets for the Parliamentarium before your visit?

1 Would you like to learn more about public events at the European Parliament? The Parliament regularly organizes events that are of interest to members of the public. You can watch all public events online via live streaming, in real time. They include plenaries and committee meetings, plus special events like press conferences. When interpretation is available, you can listen to the broadcast in all the EU's official languages. To find out more, visit the European Parliament information office in your country or go to its website.

2 No trip to Strasbourg would be complete without a visit to the European Parliament. The Parliament's Information Office in France organises guided tours whenever there is no plenary session running in Strasbourg. You'll be given a look into several different areas of the modern parliament building, including the famous meeting chamber. Tours are usually available in French, German or English. They are open to anyone aged 14 or over.

3 The Parliamentarium is the European Parliament's visitor centre: the place to go to find out all about the Parliament, its history and how it works. Located in the Parliament's Espace Leopold complex in Brussels, the centre brings together exhibits, photos and videos that explain the Parliament and the other institutions of the European Union in an engaging way. Visits are suitable for school groups, families and individuals – and they don't cost a cent. There's no need to book in advance or even bring your ID card.

4 *Step Inside:* helping people back into the community

a) Scan the text and answer questions 1–6. Use your own words if possible. Write complete sentences in your exercise book. First mark keywords.

1 What is different about the clothes sold in the shop?
2 Why was it a good idea to start a shop?
3 What is the shop's location like?
4 What was the advantage for the students who helped Phil?
5 How many people has the charity helped get back into work this year?
6 Why do people in the area like the shop?

The new *Step Inside* boutique in Greenside Avenue might look like any other high-end clothes store, but there's one key difference: all the store's products are used. *Step Inside* was the brainchild of Phil Owens, a volunteer who works with local homeless charity *The Dale Centre*, which gives people forced to sleep rough a bed for the night during the freezing winter months. "*The Dale Centre* regularly receives donations of second-hand clothes and other items, and we can't always use all of them, so starting a shop seemed like the obvious solution," explains Phil. He found an empty shop in Greenside Avenue. "It's such a beautiful area with lovely shops, and I wanted ours to fit in with the others, so I decided to make it really smart. I asked a few local art students to get involved, and they did a marvellous job. When they'd finished, it looked like a designer store! It was the best thing we could have done, because by making it look great, we attracted large numbers of customers when we opened last month."

The students benefited too, adds Phil: "They had taken photos while working on the shop, and I said it would make a good project. So they told their college about it, and in the end, they were allowed to use the photos for their end-of-year design project. And they got top marks!"

The shop is run by a team of volunteers, and every penny it makes is invested in the work of *The Dale Centre*, which has already helped over 2,200 people to find a new home this year and almost 800 to find a job again. "The great thing about the shop is that we can also offer part-time volunteer positions to homeless people who need work experience or want to get back into the world of work," adds Phil. "And we give them clothes for job interviews. Local residents have told us how pleased they are, too, because they now have somewhere nearby where they can take their preloved clothes, and they feel good knowing that they're supporting a good cause."

b) What do the underlined words mean? Write the translations in your exercise book.

c) Explain what the *Step Inside* project does in your own words. Write about 50–100 words in your exercise book.

d) Would you buy used clothes from this shop or a similar one? Why (not)? Write about 50 words in your exercise book.

Check: Reading

a) Vergleiche deine Antworten mit den Lösungen auf Seite 79 im Workbook.
b) Schätze deine Antworten mit einem grünen oder roten Gesicht ein.

		☺	☹	
1	Konntest du in Aufgabe 3 *skimmen* und dadurch den richtigen Text finden?	○	○	→ 1a
2	Konntest du in Aufgabe 3 *scannen* und dadurch in b) schnell die richtigen Antworten finden?	○	○	→ 2a
3	Konntest du in Aufgabe 4 wichtige *keywords/phrases* im Text erkennen und markieren?	○	○	→ 2a
4	Konntest du in Aufgabe 4 mit Hilfe deiner *keywords* die Fragen richtig beantworten?	○	○	→ 2a
5	Konntest du in 4b) die Wörter leicht erschließen oder im Wörterbuch schnell finden?	○	○	→ 1b
6	Konntest du in 4c) die wichtigsten Informationen des Textes entnehmen und schriftlich zusammenfassen?	○	○	→ 1d

c) Wenn du dich rot eingeschätzt hast, schau dir die rechte Spalte an. Die Nummern führen dich zu den passenden Übungen im Skills Training (S. 28–29). Dort kannst du gezielt Reading trainieren.

1 Recommended by bloggers ➔ SF 1, 11, 35 (pp. 56, 61, 73)

TIP: You skim the text to find out the main information. You scan to find details in part of the text with the help of keywords.

a) Skim the texts. What is the blog about? Circle A, B or C.

A Easter gifts **B** Lifestyle tips for vegans **C** Fashion and make-up

We never wear leather. That used to mean no alternatives except for ugly plastic fabrics. But now that the vegan community has become bigger and more mainstream, designers of clothes, shoes and accessories are using all kinds of weird and wonderful materials to create synthetic leather products that look and feel more natural. As the new Spring/Summer season is about to start, we've been looking at some of the latest innovations. From amazing pineapple-leather sneakers to trendy shoulder bags made of paper to beautiful sandals made from 'ocean leather' (that's seaweed to you and me), there are plenty of better alternatives coming onto the market now. As well as being vegan – which is obviously our main concern – they're also much better for the environment. The animal-leather processing industry produces a lot of waste and pollution, but these new fabrics are all plant-based – just like our food. We've put together a shopping guide, just in time for the Easter holidays …

Hoping to receive some make-up, creams or other beauty products as an Easter gift? Just make sure they're safe as well as cruelty-free.

Make-up and other beauty treatments have been used for thousands of years, but in the past few hundred years, in particular, they have contained dangerous cocktails of chemicals. Did you know that in 1760 an Irish countess who died prematurely – aged just 27 – was described as a 'victim of cosmetics'? She wore make-up full of toxic chemicals, which got into her blood and killed her. Luckily, today's women (and men!) can easily find natural creams, lotions, gels, etc. that make them look good without damaging their health. Best of all, in our opinion, they are often vegan. So, if you'd like your Easter treats to include honey-free, milk-free beauty products that are safe and aren't tested on animals, this is what we recommend…

This week, we've been testing five of the best Easter lunch options to make sure that animal-lovers don't have to eat boring food during the holidays. From nut roast to glazed roast vegetables to sweet bunny cupcakes that are completely free from dairy products, we have plenty of recipe ideas for vegan Easter dishes. New recipes we've tried and loved include a tasty spinach quiche, a delicious cashew cheese lasagne and a mouth-watering pecan and mushroom Wellington. It seems that meat-free, dairy-free treats are trendy this spring, and we're certainly not complaining. Who says Easter has to be tough for the vegan community?

b) Mark these words in the text. Then find the correct German translations. Write in your exercise book.

1 accessories	4 glazed	7 beauty products
2 concern	5 bunny	8 cruelty-free
3 plant-based	6 mouth-watering	9 prematurely

TIP: Before you use a dictionary, consider the context, whether you know a similar word in English, German, French, Latin or any other languages, and whether there are clues in the pictures. If you do use a dictionary, choose the meaning that best fits the context.

c) In your exercise book, list the things found in food and beauty products that the blog's authors want to avoid.

d) Summarize each text in one sentence in your exercise book.

2 A book review: *Chocky* ➔ SF 1, 12 (pp. 56, 62)

a) First read the questions and mark important words.
Then scan the text for the answers.
Write short answers in your exercise book.
Use your own words where possible.

TIP: Mark the keywords in the questions and look for them or similar words when you scan. Then read around the keywords to find the answers. Remember to look for different words or phrases with the same meaning.

1 What do Mr and Mrs Gore think about the situation with Chocky at first?
2 What basic things does Matthew tell his friend about?
3 What does Chocky hope to do?
4 Name two things that Matthew is now able to do well.
5 What makes the book different to others of the same genre?
6 Name one thing the writer of the review doesn't like about the novel.

An engaging page-turner with an important message

Chocky by John Wyndham is a short novel published in 1968. It tells the unusual story of 12-year-old Matthew Gore, who has a friend that only he can see. At first, his parents think he is a little old to behave like this, but they don't see any reason to do anything. However, they start to worry after hearing Matthew's conversations with his friend in which he explains that a week has seven days and the human race has males and females. At school, Matthew starts asking strange questions in maths lessons, and suddenly gets the best marks in science. He explains to his worried parents that this friend, Chocky, is a super-intelligent alien being who has come to Earth from a distant planet to learn about how everything works, with the hope of helping humans to improve the way they live and look after the planet that they call home.

Mr and Mrs Gore find it difficult to believe their son's explanation, but all the signs are there: Matthew saves his sister from drowning even though he has never been a good swimmer, and he wins prizes for painting even though he had never been good at art before. It appears that he is receiving help. His parents decide they need a medical opinion, and a visit to a psychiatrist confirms that the boy does seem to be in communication with something. Could it be that Chocky isn't just inside his head? The government is informed about the situation, and then things start to become dangerous for Matthew and his family.

Wyndham wrote several other famous works of science fiction, including *Day of the Triffids*, but compared with them – and most other novels from this genre – this is a very heart-warming book, even though the story might seem creepy at first. Both the way in which Mr Gore shows that he cares about his son and his gentle attitude towards the situation are lovely. And Chocky is not what you would expect from an alien visitor: she (Matthew says that on Chocky's planet there are no sexes, but Chocky sounds more like a 'she') is kind and is also worried about Matthew's safety, which is why she leaves at the end of the book.

The novel is forward-looking in the way that it raises questions about our terrible attitude towards the environment and the way we consume energy, as well as the corruption in our governments and societies. Being a 1960s novel, the gender roles described by Wyndham – as well as some of the characters' ways of speaking – seem rather old-fashioned now, but this was my only problem with the book. All in all, this is a gripping and thought-provoking read whose message is still relevant, given the way many people are unthinkingly destroying our amazing, beautiful planet.

b) Read the text in detail, then look at the guidelines for writing book reviews on pp. 41–43 of your student's book. Did this writer follow all the guidelines? Write 100–150 words in your exercise book explaining what you would improve.

c) Would you like to read the novel? Why (not)? Write 100–150 words in your exercise book.

How is the world changing?

1 Past, present, future ➜ SB (pp. 52–53) • SF 31 (pp. 71–72)

Use the pictures to think about how technology will affect shopping in the future. Make notes and discuss with a partner the advantages and disadvantages of online shopping.
What might happen if we all ordered everything for delivery by drone?

Photo 1 shows ... Picture 2 shows ...
The advantages/disadvantages are ...
If everything were delivered by drone, we would ...

1

2

2 Your world – your future ➜ SB (p. 53) • SF 27 (p. 70)

a) 17 What is the main topic of the conversation between Colin and his daughter Emily? Circle the correct answer.

A relationships in the past and now **B** online safety **C** how Emily's parents met

b) 17 Now read the questions. Then listen again and write down the answers.

1 Write down three things that happened on Colin's date with Mary.

– ____________________

– ____________________

– ____________________

2 How does Colin describe dating? ____________________

____

3 Do Emily's friends chat with their dates on their phones? ____________________

____

4 What does Emily's dad warn her can happen at parties? ____________________

____

5 What happened at the party last month? ____________________

____

6 What does Colin say about sharing photos? ____________________

____

3 WORDS Robo-journalism ➜ SB (pp. 54–55)

Complete the text with words from the box in the correct form. You will not need all the words.

artificial · complex · concerned about · deal with · delivery · depend on · election · future · information · package · progress · replace · risk · robot · survival · waste

The benefits of artificial (1) intelligence still have to be seen in many areas, but in one sphere there has already been some progress. Journalists might well need to be worried that they're going to be replaced (2) by machines very soon. Specially programmed robots (3) are able to write quite complex (4) articles automatically without any human intervention, and there are already several American companies selling news written by a computer. The software looks through internet updates to find information (5) and can then 'write' a short text based on previous articles. The quality of the output, of course, depends on (6) the correctness of the information, and there is always the risk (7) of serious error. We already believe computer-generated bots can affect the result of ~~progress~~ elections (8). Journalists don't need to be concerned about (9) their jobs just yet, although computers could pose a threat to the ~~progress~~ survival (10) of their jobs in the future (11).

4 REVISION What might happen in the future (The definite article) ➜ SB (p. 56)

a) Look at p. 192 of your book and read about the use of the definite article in English. Then look at the following words and tick (✓) where the definite article is needed.

1 ◯ science
2 ◯ dictionary
3 ◯ living in a city
4 ◯ most of the students
5 ◯ Greek food
6 ◯ future

b) Decide where you need to add a definite article to the sentences below.

1 I believe ________ people will be replaced by ________ robots in many jobs in the future.

2 ________ technological progress we have seen over the last few years has been extremely fast.

3 ________ unemployment[1] will grow because ________ computers will do our jobs.

4 Almost every computer on ________ planet is connected to ________ internet nowadays.

5 In my school, everyone thinks ________ packages will be delivered by ________ drones in the future.

6 ________ most crops[2] need bees to help pollinate[3] them.

7 Without ________ bees, we would have no honey, no kiwi fruit and no coffee.

8 What can we do to help ________ insects that are having problems surviving ________ climate change?

9 Deep in a mountain in ________ Arctic between Norway and ________ North Pole, there is a "seed bank" where ________ scientists can store plants to protect them against dying out.

10 ________ scientists working there have to survive some very difficult conditions and ________ extreme temperatures.

[1]unemployment [ˌʌnɪmˈplɔɪmənt] *Arbeitslosigkeit* [2]crop [ˈkrɒp] *(Feld-)Frucht* [3]pollinate [ˈpɒləneɪt] *bestäuben*

5 REVISION The web never forgets (Sequence of adverbials) ➔ SB (p. 56)

Rewrite the sentences including the adverbials.

1 Think before posting something embarrassing on social media. (carefully, potentially[1])

2 There have been cases of young people posting videos of bullying. (lately, on the web)

3 A 13-year-old girl from North Wales became upset after someone uploaded a video. (extremely, in September 2017)

4 Only classmates saw it, but it went viral. (at first, quickly)

5 Arriving at school, they found two police officers waiting in the classroom. (patiently, the next morning)

6 The girl's mother had become so angry that she reported the class to the police. (the night before, immediately)

7 The police decided that there wasn't enough evidence[2]. (in the end, really)

8 The school decided to take action and punished the whole class. (finally, instead)

9 We will find out who uploaded the video. (probably, to the web, unfortunately, never)

[1] potentially [pə'tenʃəli] möglicherweise [2] evidence ['evɪdəns] Beweis

b) ● Arrange the following sentences containing adverbs in the right order and highlight the adverbs.

1 almost · a mobile phone · Today · and upload · and can take · everyone has · to the internet · images

2 with that · we're doing · always · think · The danger · carefully · about what · is we don't

3 quickly · and millions of people · Photos can · we even realise · can see them · before · go viral

4 often · to check · It's important · and your photos are · are OK · that your settings · properly protected

5 to check · you still need · can see your messages · regularly · that only people you want · you're careful · Even if

6 so don't · just add everyone · become a big problem · Unfortunately · to a website · who invites you · cyber-bullying · has

7 immediately · delete it · If a friend · quickly · so they can · tell them · posts something they shouldn't

8 many problems · forever · but a photo · Luckily · can stay · are forgotten · in the cyberworld · quickly

c) Imagine you are giving advice to younger students when joining a new social media site. Think of what's important to remember when giving out personal information. Write a paragraph giving at least five internet safety tips in your exercise book. Use a variety of different adverbs and the following words or your own words:

be careful · check if · don't meet · never give out · your address

6 ACCESS TO WORDS Staying connected ➜ SB (p. 57)

a) What can you do in the following situations? Use a verb from box A and a suitable noun (or phrase) from box B and write the collocations below. There may be several correct options.

A

block · browse · charge · click on · customize · delete · enter · export · increase · manage · open · press · replace · swipe

B

a new tab · a phrase in the search bar · the attachment · the battery · the button · the icon · the web · to a different format · unwanted friend requests · your card · your computer's memory · your contact list · your phone · your settings

b) Now go through the collocations from a) and write ten or more sentences using them.

1 *If some programs start to run slowly, you can increase your computer's memory.*

7 Feature article ➜ SB (pp. 58–60) • SF 1–2 (p. 56)

a) How many different crops do you know? Make a mind map in your exercise book using vegetable, fruit and grain as umbrella words.

b) Read the text, add ideas to your mind map and sum up its message in two sentences.

SOS – Save our seeds!

No matter where you go, every supermarket seems to have the same fruit and vegetables. Go to the market and you might find a bit more variety, but it still won't come close to the range of different foods the older generation used to enjoy. Maybe some of your grandparents' favourite childhood foods don't even exist any more.

Vegetables, just like clothes, go in and out of fashion. Until not long ago, people would grow their own food in the garden, and they would carefully plant and harvest their own 'mini' crops all year round. Because of our hectic and urban lifestyles, people just aren't producing their own vegetables any more, and the farmers who put food on our tables are turning to higher-yield[1] crops to maximize profit. A 1999 study carried out by the UN's Food and Agriculture Organization (FAO) revealed that over the last century, 75 % of agricultural crops have been lost. The result is that today, 75 % of the world's food is limited to just 12 species of plant. When people don't grow crops, the seeds become worthless.

Scientists who were horrified by the idea of losing this diversity started discussions in the 1980s about what could be done. The result was the opening, in 2008, of the Svalbard Global Seed Vault[2] on the Norwegian island of Spitsbergen located in the Arctic Ocean. The idea was to set up a permanent 'library' holding a backup copy of seeds stored in different gene banks all over the world. In the event of war, bad management or something as simple as a broken freezer, there would be a duplicate in Norway so that there is always a surviving seed somewhere on the planet.

Since opening a decade ago, over 5,000 species and 890,000 seed samples have been brought to the island. The Vault itself can hold over 4.5 million seed samples, and each sample can contain an average of 500 seeds, so there is still plenty of room available.

Lots of different governments and research centres work closely with the Norwegian Ministry of Agriculture and Food, the Nordic Genetic Resource Centre (NordGen) and the Crop Trust in Germany, which run the facility, to store seeds for future generations. They do this in the Vault, which is housed in a mountain and which remains at a constant −18° Celsius. Because it is so cold deep in the mountain, even if the electricity failed or there was a problem with the Vault's systems, the seeds would stay frozen long enough to be saved. Norway's political stability will also help make sure the seeds are protected for years to come.

In an ideal world, the seeds we lock safely away in the freezing Vault will never be needed. However, one country has unfortunately already had to withdraw[3] some samples. With the escalation of conflict in Aleppo, ICARDA (The International Centre for Agricultural Research in Dry Areas) had to evacuate its Syrian office, which meant the loss of an important local resource. Luckily, they had stored a backup of nearly all their seeds in the vault in Norway. Without it, some crops may have been lost forever.

We can never be sure what is going to happen in our world, and nutritionists and scientists believe it is vital we start planning for the future now. The Global Seed Vault truly is a way to Save Our Seeds!

c) ○ Identify where you can find the different parts of the structure.

Headline l./ll. ____________ Introduction l./ll. ____________ Conclusion l./ll. ________

Summary l./ll. ____________ Main body l./ll. ____________

[1]yield [jiːld] *Ertrag* [2]vault [vɔːlt] *Tresor* [3]withdraw [wɪð'drɔː] hier: *entnehmen*

d) Read the questions. Read the text again and write short answers:

1 Why do we have less variety of food now? ______

2 What is the Global Seed Vault (GSV)? ______

3 When was it opened? ______

4 Where is the Global Seed Vault located? ______

5 How many seeds can be stored in each sample? ______

6 Which bodies work together in the GSV? ______

7 What happens if the cooling system fails? ______

8 Which country has needed to remove seeds from the GSV? ______

e) ● Find the following nouns or noun phrases in the text and match the phrases they are followed by to the terms in the box. Write the terms in the right column.

contact clause · defining relative clause · relative clause with "which" · non-defining relative clause

ll. 5–6: range of different foods ______ ______

ll. 23: Scientists ______ ______

l. 43: Crop Trust in Germany, ______ ______

l. 59: Syrian office, ______ ______

f) **Add a relative clause to give some extra information on each of the following sentences. Use your own ideas.**

1 Our lives are very hectic nowadays. *Our lives are very hectic nowadays, which leaves no time for our families and friends.*

2 Farmers now only grow 12 different species of plant. ______

3 A permanent 'library' of seeds will be stored inside an Arctic mountain. ______

4 The Vault can hold over 4.5 million samples. ______

5 These samples are kept at a constant temperature of –18° Celsius. ______

6 Norway is a very stable democracy. ______

7 The headquarters of ICARDA in Aleppo were damaged. ______

8 We cannot guarantee[1] the safety of seeds in times of war or natural disaster. ______

8 EXTRA Keeping the planet safe

→ SB (p. 63) • SF21 (p. 67) • Wordbank 4, 5

• **What do you know about different types of renewable[2] energy?**

a) **Choose one of the following technologies and present its advantages and disadvantages. Use the internet to research information and make notes.**

TIP: These words will help with your research: *wind farm, solar panel, biomass, biodiesel, (wood) pellets, offshore/onshore*

wind turbines[3]

photovoltaic panels

biomass

b) **Working in small groups, present your findings to one another.**

c) **Hold a class vote on which technology is the most interesting and promising.**

[1]guarantee sth. [ˌgærən'tiː] etwas garantieren [2]renewable [rɪ'njuːəbl] [3]turbine ['tɜːbaɪn]

9 Living to 150? 200? ➜ *SB (pp. 64–66)*

Complete the text using words and phrases from the box. You will not need all the words.

alternative · bright · *cancer* · civilization · damaging · hypothetical · imagination · immortality · physically · reasonable · recover from · science fiction · sincerely · smart

Imagine a future in which *cancer* (1) doesn't kill you. Imagine a ______ (2) world in which *nothing* kills you! Author and old-age researcher Aubrey de Grey, who has a doctorate in biology from the University of Cambridge, already believes in human ______ (3), saying it's no longer ______ (4); in fact, he ______ (5) believes that the first person who will live to the age of 150 has already been born. But is this theory ______ (6)? The British scientist argues it is the ______ (7) side effects of metabolism[1] that eventually kill us, so if we can develop ______ (8) medicines which treat issues at a genetic level rather than ______ (9), we may be able to ______ (10) deadly diseases just a few years from now. However, not all scientists agree with de Grey and do not see such a ______ (11) future for medicine: in fact, 28 leading experts (including from University College, London, and the Massachusetts Institute of Technology, US) wrote a report saying that everything is in de Grey's ______ (12), and that none of his therapies have ever worked on any living organism at all.

10 Intercultural relationships ➜ *SB (p. 67) • SF 22–25 (pp. 68–69)*

● Your English friend, Max, has sent you a link to a radio programme in German. He only speaks a little German, so he asks if you can summarize what is said.

TIP: What is the radio programme about? What does Dr Hartmann-Suarez recommend?

a) 18 Listen to the text and write down the main points.

b) Write an email to Max (100–150 words) explaining him the most important ideas covered in the interview.

11 LISTENING COURSE Gist and inference ➜ *SB (pp. 68–69) • SF 27 (p. 70)*

You will hear excerpts from five short news reports. The beginning of the report is missing, so you will have to work out what is being said from the rest of the report. You will not understand everything, but the idea is to get the gist of what is being said.

a) 19 Listen to the reports, and write down what each report is about.

1 ______

2 ______

3 ______

4 ______

5 ______

[1] metabolism [məˈtæbəlɪzəm] *Stoffwechsel*

b) ● 20 You will now hear five short texts, and you will need to read between the lines. Which of the following answers best explains the situation? (Circle) the right answer.

1 **A** The person is being invited to a meeting.
B The person needs to totally rewrite the report by Tuesday evening.
C The person can rewrite the report if they have time.

2 **A** It wasn't the best film ever.
B It wasn't a film at all.
C The film was pretty bad.

3 **A** The person will probably join you later.
B The person has too much work.
C The person will probably not come.

4 **A** The person is asking you to open a window.
B The person wants to talk about the weather with you.
C The person feels ill and wants some fresh air.

5 **A** The person is getting a holiday the next day.
B The person is losing their job.
C The person is getting a new office.

12 STUDY SKILLS Roles in a panel discussion ➜ SB (p. 70) • SF 17–19 (pp. 64–66)

Look again at the tips in section 2 b) on p. 70 of your student's book.
Match the following example phrases to the tips:

A [2] "I think that's very interesting, but we need to look at it from a slightly different point of view."

B [ ] "I'd like to first give an example, and then explain a little about my personal experience."

C [ ] "I will warn you once you get to 60 seconds, and then cut off your microphone at 1 minute and 15 seconds."

D [ ] "I've definitely found myself in the same situation, yes."

E [ ] "I believe the rich should be made to pay more tax."

F [ ] "Like the lady before me explained, this is an issue which will affect our children and grandchildren."

G [ ] "Today we'll be discussing the plans for a new turbine in Bluebell Fields. We have invited local farmers and council members."

H [ ] "We'll hear the opinions of three experts in the field to make sure we don't miss anything out."

I [ ] "We seem to have moved away a bit from the question. If we could just make sure we return to the subject of the discussion, please."

J [ ] "If we could save any questions until the end, please, to give everyone an opportunity to speak."

K [ ] "So, I'd like to open the discussion up to any questions from the audience."

L [ ] "I think this has been a very productive discussion today, so all that's left is to thank my guests on both sides."

1 PRONUNCIATION Word stress

21 Say these words from Unit 3 aloud and underline the stressed syllable. You can record your voice. Listen and check.

1 alternative	3 complex	5 digital	7 exclusive	9 (to) export	11 radioactive
2 battery	4 controversial	6 electricity	8 (an) export	10 parasite	12 vision

2 WORDS Defining words

a) Here are definitions of four new verbs which appear in this unit. Identify the verbs.

1 to stop someone doing something by law *to ban*

2 to pause for a short time ______

3 to connect a mobile phone to the electricity supply ______

4 to take one thing out and put another one in ______

b) Here are four more new verbs from the unit. Write your own definition for each one.

1 to depend on *to rely on*

2 to deliver ______

3 to recover ______

4 to predict ______

3 Using adverbs

Rewrite the following sentences, turning the underlined words or phrases into adverbs. You might need to make changes to word order, etc.

1 The government has had to introduce an immediate ban on this.

The government has had to ban this immediately.

2 New species mean that we can make more economic use of resources.

______

3 Luckily the patient made a complete recovery.

______

4 We only have a vague understanding of the threat this issue might cause.

______

5 Could you please give a concise explanation of what the issue is?

______

6 It is my sincere hope we can come to an agreement on this matter.

______

	Jack	Sara	Marcus
Height	Do you know Jack? He's pretty tall (for his age, at least).	I want to tell you about Sara. Her **height** is average, neither tall nor short,	Here's a photo of Marcus. He's a bit **on the short side**,
Build	He says he's **skinny**; I'd describe him as thin, about average build but not that **muscular**, it's true.	and she's quite athletic – **slim** and **toned**.	and kind of **stocky**. I wouldn't say fat or chubby, but definitely fairly **chunky** in a nice way, with
Hair	His hair is medium-length and **wavy** brown, but it used to be much longer.	The first thing you notice is her long blond dreadlocks, and **dyed** hair – bits of pink today!	short **frizzy** black hair and a short beard and **moustache** too. He's worried about going bald, but I think it's more that
Face	His face is long, with high **cheek-bones**, and you won't find a more	Sara says her face is **chubby**; I think it's round and **suits** her. Her ears are **pierced**, of course, and she's very	his **forehead** is high! There's always a smile on his face – you can't imagine anyone more **cheerful** and ready for a
Character	relaxed person. I think you'd like him. At times, Jack can be rather **vain**. For example, he has glasses, but **rarely** wears them, because he can be **disorganized**. On the other hand, people agree he's an easy-going sort of person who's also very hard-working. Everyone says Jack's the calm but confident type, though not always terribly reliable.	cool. Although she **gives the impression of** being very **outgoing**, she's in fact not that confident and once told me she often feels shy in company. It's true Sara's not always very talkative, but you'd never describe her as boring. There's a serious side to her too – she's a great reader.	laugh. At the same time, he's really creative and is into music and art in a big way. His **ambition** is to be a DJ, which is something he's very serious about. Marcus **comes across as** someone who's friendly and always ready to help. It's great to have him as a friend: I've found him to be patient and a really good listener.
Clothes	His style is smart casual – you know, jeans and T-shirts but I've seen him in a suit and he looked really good in it.	Her style in clothes shows her **sporty** nature: trainers and **tracksuit** bottoms are the norm. She **tends to** wear darker colours. That makes her hair **stand out** even more!	**In terms of** clothing, you're most likely to find him in loose and **baggy** clothes and not choosing a weird creative appearance, if you know what I mean.

Write a short description of a famous person or someone you know, but don't give the name. Can your partner guess who your person is?

TIP: Be sensitive, polite and less direct than you might be if writing in German.
~~He's very fat.~~ He's a bit on the heavy side.
~~She is nervous.~~ She gives the impression of being nervous.

Height: height [haɪt] *(Körper)Größe* **He's on the short/fat/… side.** *Er ist eher klein/dick/…* **Build: build** *Körperbau* **chunky** *stämmig* **muscular** ['mʌskjələ] *muskulös* **skinny** *abgemagert* **slim** *schlank* **stocky** *pummelig* **toned** [təʊnd] *fit, stark* **Hair: dyed** [daɪd] *gefärbt* **forehead** ['fɔːhed, 'fɒrɪd] *Stirn* **frizzy** *kraus* **moustache** [mə'stɑːʃ] *Schnurrbart* **wavy** ['weɪvi] *wellig* **Face: cheekbone** ['tʃiːkbəʊn] *Wangenknochen* **chubby** *pausbäckig* **pierced** *durchlocht, gepierct* **(to) suit sb.** *jm. passen* **Character: ambition** [æm'bɪʃn] *Ambition, Ehrgeiz* **cheerful** ['tʃɪəfl] *heiter* **(to) come across as sth.** *als etwas wirken* **disorganized** [dɪs'ɔːgənaɪzd] *schlecht organisiert, chaotisch* **(to) give the impression of doing sth.** *den Eindruck machen/vermitteln, etwas zu tun* **outgoing** ['aʊtgəʊɪŋ] *aus sich herausgehend, extrovertiert* **rarely** ['reəli] *selten* **vain** [veɪn] *eitel* **Clothes: baggy** *ausgebeult* **in terms of …** *Was … angeht/betrifft* **norm** *Regel* **sporty** ['spɔːti] *sportlich, sportbegeistert* **(to) stand out** *auffallen* **(to) tend to do sth.** *dazu neigen, etwas zu tun* **tracksuit bottoms** *(pl)* ['træksuːt ˌbɒtəmz] *Jogginghose*

Fotos: Shutterstock (Jack: Milles Studio; Sara: PHB.cz (Richard Semik); Marcus: Akhenaton Images)

1 Making requests

2 Asking for information and help

battery *Akku* **(to) charge** *aufladen* **autograph** *Autogramm* **Could you spare a minute** *Hättest du eine Minute?*
I don't suppose you could … *Du könntest wohl nicht für mich …?*

 Illustrationen: Christian Bartz, Berlin

3 Saying what you would and wouldn't like to do

Making plans

What I'd really love to do is see that new James Bond film. Do you want to come with me?

Thanks for asking, but I'm **not that keen** on action movies, actually. What about eating out?

Another idea …

I wouldn't mind trying that new Chinese restaurant.

I'm not a big fan of Chinese food, actually.

Or …

Actually, I wouldn't mind watching sport on TV for a while. What do you think?

I'd rather not do that, to be honest. **I'm not too fond of** watching TV in the day time.

Or …

But I wouldn't mind an afternoon in town. We could have a look in the shops and maybe get some new shoes.

I would rather you didn't take me to any more shoe shops, to be honest. How about going for a coffee somewhere?

Or …

A coffee **would be** wonderful. How about that place by the park? Or the new one in the shopping centre?

I don't have strong feelings either way.

4 Saying someone is wrong or mistaken

I'd rather … ['rɑːðə] *Ich würde lieber …* **(to) be fond of sth.** *etwas gerne haben* **I would rather …** *Ich möchte lieber …* **idiot** ['ɪdiət] *Idiot/in* **satellite** ['sætəlaɪt] *Satellit* **unmanned** *unbesetzt* **mission** ['mɪʃn] *Mission* **absolutely** *unbedingt*

Illustrationen: Christian Bartz, Berlin

Wordbank 3: Electoral systems

First, you have to be 18 or older, then you have to register in the **constituency** where you live. UK citizens have the right to vote, as well as Irish and Commonwealth citizens living in the UK. In England, there are elections to the House of Commons, the European Parliament and local **councils**. Some cities also elect their police and crime **commissioners**.
The most important election is the General Election to the House of Commons, which by law has to take place every five years. Anybody can stand for election to parliament if they can make a £500 **deposit** and find 10 people to support them. Candidates who don't reach a 5 % **threshold** don't get their deposit back.
Polling day is always on a Thursday. Voters either go to their local polling station, send a postal vote, or ask a friend to vote **by proxy**.
Polling stations are open from 7 am to 10 pm. You give their name to the people there (we have no ID cards here!), and their name is crossed off the list.
Then you go into a voting **booth** and mark the **ballot paper** with just one cross next to the name of the candidate you want to vote for. You then put the paper into the ballot box.
At 10 pm, the boxes are taken to a counting location in each constituency, often a sports hall, and the votes are counted. When this is over, the **Returning Officer** announces the winner.
The General Election uses a "first past the post" system, which means that only one candidate is elected as MP for the constituency. This often means that MPs are elected with less than 50 % of the vote.
The party with the most MPs (out of 650) forms the new government.

ballot paper ['bælət] Stimmzettel **booth** [buːð] *Kabine* **by proxy** ['prɒksi] *mit Vollmacht* **constituency** [kən'stɪtjuənsi] *Wahlkreis* **deposit** [dɪ'pɒzɪt] *Pfand* **police and crime commissioner** [kə'mɪʃənə] ≈ *Polizeipräsident/in* **polling** ['pəʊlɪŋ] *Wählen, Wahl* **Returning Officer** *Wahlleiter/in* **threshold** ['θreʃhəʊld] *Hürde*

We Americans have to be 18 or over to vote, and we have to register first.
If you can't or don't want to go to the polling station on Election Day, you can vote via an **absentee ballot**, which you send by post. In some states you can choose "early voting": you go to the polling station before Election Day. 36 % chose this option in the 2016 presidential election.
Voters usually **cast** their ballots with scanning machines (with a pen) or electronic machines (with buttons or a touchscreen).
Federal elections are for the House of Representatives (435 members elected for 2 years) and the Senate (100 members elected for 6 years).
The presidential election is different: each of the 50 states chooses **Electors**. States with larger populations have more Electors, smaller states fewer (California has 55, eight states have only 3). The members of the Electoral **College** vote for the presidential candidate who won the highest number of popular votes in their state. This "winner takes all" system means that a candidate can be elected president with fewer popular votes nationwide than their **opponent**. This has happened five times in US history: in 1824, 1876, 1888, 2000 and 2016.
There are also state elections (e. g. for governor) and local elections (e. g. at city level, for mayor and city councils).

absentee ballot [æbsən'tiː] *Briefwahl* **(to) cast** [kɑːst] *abgeben* **college** ['kɒlɪdʒ] *(Wahl)Kollegium* **elector** [ɪ'lektə] *Wahlmann, -frau* **opponent** [ə'pəʊnənt] *Gegner/in*

Use these notes or your own experiences and write an explanation of the German electoral system.

In der Bundesrepublik gibt es neben Wahlen zum Europäischen Parlament drei verschiedene Wahlen. Bei den Kommunalwahlen geht es um die niedrigste Ebene, also um die Gemeinde oder den Stadtbezirk. In jedem Bundesland gibt es ein unterschiedliches Wahlrecht. Die Landesparlamente haben verschiedene Namen. Hier werden MdL, MdA, MdBB bzw. MdHB gewählt. Mitglieder der jeweiligen Landesregierungen sind im Bundesrat vertreten.
Die Bundestagswahl findet alle vier Jahre statt. Zwei Besonderheiten sind in Deutschland wichtig: die Erst-/Zweitstimme und die Fünfprozenthürde. Die Erststimme geht an eine Person. Wer die meisten Stimmen bekommt, erhält ein Direktmandat und wird MdB seines Wahlkreises, von denen es zurzeit 299 gibt. Die Zweitstimme geht an eine Partei, sodass die Sitzverteilung der Parteien dem Anteil ihrer Wahlstimmen entspricht.
Die Fünfprozenthürde verhindert die Wahl einer Vielzahl kleinerer Parteien in den Bundestag: Parteien, die weniger als 5 % aller Stimmen bekommen, dürfen nicht ins Parlament einziehen, es sei denn, mindestens drei ihrer Kandidat/innen wurden im Wahlkreis direkt gewählt.

1 Energy generation

windmill

coal mining

oil drilling

hydroelectric plant

geothermal energy

nuclear reactor

solar power

wind farm

Thanks to the invention of the solar cell, we can now **make use of** the sun's power as a source of green energy.
We are not as dependent on fossil fuels, which cause pollution.

2 Transport

wheel

locomotive

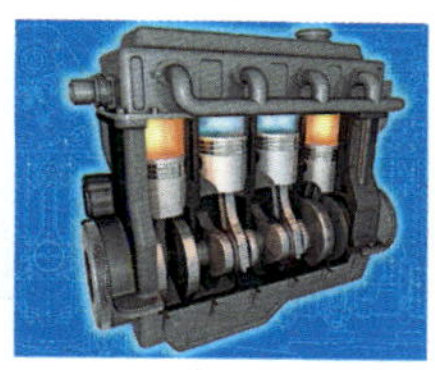
combustion engine

mass-produced cars

commercial flights

space shuttle

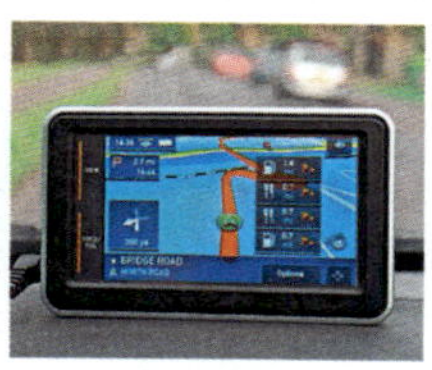
sat(ellite) nav(igation)

electric car

The invention of the locomotive and later the internal combustion engine **made it possible** for people to travel faster and for longer distances than riding or walking. **One of the positive effects of this** was that the world became smaller and mass travel **became possible**.

3 Household

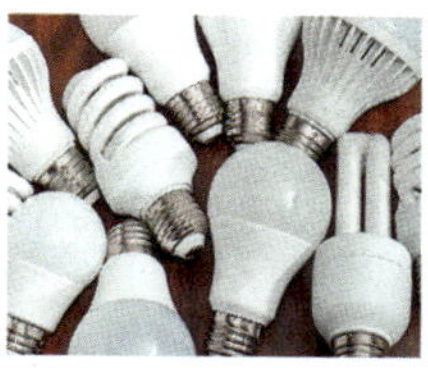
electric light

washing machine

radio

fridge

TV

microwave oven

home computer

smart home

The impact of the washing machine **cannot be overstated. It allowed** millions of women to enter the world of work as they no longer needed to spend most of the week washing the family's clothes.
One of the negative effects was that millions of maids lost their jobs.

combustion [kəmˈbʌstʃən] *Verbrennung* **commercial flight** [kəˈmɜːʃl] *Passagier-, Linienflug* **(to) drill** *bohren* **fossil fuel** [ˈfɒsl ˌfjuːəl] *fossiler Brennstoff* **geothermal energy** [ˌdʒiːəʊˈθɜːml] *Erdwärme* **hydroelectric plant** [ˌhaɪdrəʊɪˈlektrɪk] *Wasserkraftwerk* **invention** [ɪnˈvenʃn] *Erfindung* **locomotive** [ˌləʊkəˈməʊtɪv] **maid** [meɪd] *Dienstmädchen* **(to) overstate** [ˌəʊvəˈsteɪt] *überbewerten* **space shuttle** [ˈʃʌtl] *Raumfähre* **solar** [ˈsəʊlə]

Fotos: Shutterstock (Reihe 1, Bild 1: Fredy Thuerig, 2: Rasta777, 3: QiuJu Song, 4: ZoranOrcik, 5: N.Minton; R. 2, 1: nixki, 2: Wang An Qi, 3: WDG Photo; R. 3, 1: Lightspring, 2: jgorzynik, 3: Nikonaft, 4: Evgeniya Chertova, 5: BlueRingMedia; R. 4, 1: Dsculptor, 2: jennyt, 3: Nerthuz; R. 5, 1: anmbph, 2: Pro3DArtt, 3: Africa Studio, 4: Iconic Bestiary, 5: Dja65; R. 6, 1: MrGarry, 2: horiyan, 3: Brian A Jackson)

4 Telecommunications

telegraph

telephone

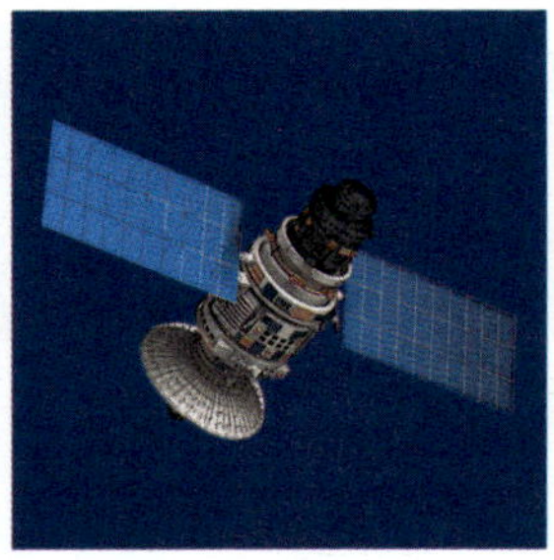
satellite

www

email

mobile phone

SMS

smartphone

The main benefit of mobile phones is that they have **made it possible** for people to stay in touch and find and send information wherever they are in the world. This **has had a huge influence on** how people communicate.

5 Agriculture

pasteurization

tractor

industrial greenhouse

combine harvester

pesticides

frozen foods

GM foods

agricultural drone

The invention of fertilizer and pesticides **enabled** farmers to increase the productivity of their land dramatically and to support the growing population of their country.

combine harvester [ˌkɒmbaɪn ˈhɑːvɪstə] *Mähdrescher* **fertilizer** [ˈfɜːtəlaɪzə] *Düngemittel* **GM (genetically modified)** *gentechnisch verändert* **influence** *Einfluss* **pasteurization** [ˌpɑːstʃəraɪˈzeɪʃn] *Pasteurisierung* **pesticide** [ˈpestɪsaɪd] **satellite** [ˈsætəlaɪt]

Fotos: Shutterstock (Reihe 1, Bild 1: rook76, 2: Frannyanne, 3: Phonlamai Photo, 4: atm2003; R. 2, 1: Titov Nikolai, 2: Vangert, 3: Fine Art, 4: Es sarawuth; R. 3, 1: Mega Pixel, 2: ShendArt, 3: gtfour, 4: Orientaly; R. 4, 1: Adriano Kirihara, 2: defotoberg, 3: Alex_Traksel, 4: Suwin)

Causes

- Burning **fossil fuels** in power stations
- **Carbon dioxide emissions** from transport
- **Deforestation**, legal and illegal
- Use of electricity and **resources** in industry and **manufacturing**
- Use of **chemical fertilizers** in farming
- **Methane** from cows and rice fields
- **Drilling** for **oil** and other natural resources
- Unnecessary **consumption**: shopping and using resources
- Waste: rubbish that is **dumped** after human use

Consequences

- Melting polar ice cap
- Rising sea levels
- Rising sea temperatures
- **Extreme** weather: prolonged **heatwaves**, droughts, wildfires, and floods
- Crop **failure** and food **shortages**
- Death of coral reefs
- Health problems
- Increasing **income inequality** as the poor cannot **afford** higher prices for products and resources
- Conflict and wars between countries over resources
- Loss of animal habitat leading to **extinction**

What governments can do

- Promote the use of alternative, greener and **sustainable** sources of energy: wind and **solar** power, **tidal** energy
- Increase **investment** in greener transport systems, **decommission power stations**
- International **cooperation** to fight pollution, overuse of resources and to protect wildlife
- Develop strategies to reduce human and industrial waste, and to increase recycling
- Introduce heavy fines for industrial pollution and waste
- Reduce or ban the use of chemical fertilizers and pesticides

What individuals can do

- Form pressure groups to demand changes in the law
- Participate in peaceful protests, take part in marches and join campaigns to put pressure on governments and increase **awareness** of the issue
- Reduce your **carbon footprint**: buy less, recycle more, avoid products with unnecessary **packaging**, and share transport, or ride a bike to school or work
- Choose energy-**efficient lighting** and eat less meat

Make a list of three things you **already** do to reduce your carbon footprint, and add two more you **could** do:

________________ ________________ ________________

________________ ________________

(to) afford sth. [ə'fɔːd] *sich etwas leisten* **awareness** [ə'weənəs] *Bewusstsein* **carbon dioxide** [ˌkɑːbən daɪ'ɒksaɪd] *Kohlendioxid* **carbon footprint** CO_2-Fußabdruck **chemical fertilizer** ['fɜːtəlaɪzə] *chemisches Düngemittel* **consequence** ['kɒnsɪkwəns] *Folge* **consumption** [kən'sʌmpʃn] *Verbrauch* **cooperation** [kəʊˌɒpə'reɪʃn] *Zusammenarbeit* **(to) decommission** [ˌdiːkə'mɪʃn] *stilllegen* **deforestation** [ˌdiːˌfɒrɪ'steɪʃn] *Abholzung* **(to) drill** *bohren* **(to) dump** *abladen* **efficient** [ɪ'fɪʃnt] *effizient* **emission** [i'mɪʃn] *Ausstoß* **extinction** [ɪk'stɪŋkʃn] *Aussterben* **extreme** [ɪk'striːm] *extrem* **failure** ['feɪljə] *Ausfall* **fossil fuel** ['fɒsl fjuːəl] *fossiler Brennstoff* **heatwave** ['hiːtweɪv] *Hitzewelle* **income** ['ɪnkʌm] *Einkommen* **inequality** [ˌɪnɪ'kwɒləti] *Ungleichheit* **investment** [ɪn'vestmənt] *Investition* **lighting** *Beleuchtung* **manufacturing** [ˌmænju'fæktʃərɪŋ] *Fertigung* **methane** ['miːθeɪn] *Methan* **oil** [ɔɪl] *Öl* **packaging** ['pækɪdʒɪŋ] *Verpackung* **power station** ['steɪʃn] *Kraftwerk* **prolonged** [prə'lɒŋd] *anhaltend* **resources** *(pl)* [rɪ'sɔːsɪz] *Ressourcen* **shortage** ['ʃɔːtɪdʒ] *Knappheit* **solar** ['səʊlə] *Sonnen-* **sustainable** [sə'steɪnəbl] erneuerbar, *nachhaltig* **tidal** ['taɪdl] *Gezeiten-*

Foto: Shutterstock/Photomontage

Wordbank 6: Films

Talking about genres

- I really like nature documentaries.
- There was a really good documentary on TV last night.
- It was **fascinating**.

- I just love thrillers.
- *Vertigo* is a **classic**
- It's really gripping.

- Comedies are my favourite.
- There's a really good one on tonight.
- It's hilarious. It really made me laugh.

- I quite enjoy adventure films.
- The latest *Indiana Jones* is good fun.
- It's really exciting and very **imaginative**.

- I really enjoy **sci-fi** movies.
- I could watch them all day.
- I find them **thought-provoking**.

- I **can't stand** horror films.
- I couldn't sleep after watching *Dracula*.
- It's really scary.

- I saw a brilliant superhero film last night.
- I've seen *Spiderman* at least ten times.
- It's really **action-packed**.

- I'm not really into war films.
- I don't enjoy them at all.
- They're too **violent**.

- You can't beat a good musical.
- They're great fun.
- They're so enjoyable.

- I'm really into **romcoms**.
- They're great entertainment.
- They can be really **heart-warming** too.

Talking about films

- The film's about …
- The plot was really interesting / a bit **unbelievable**.
- The film is set in London in the 1960s.

Talking about the actors and characters

- The main characters are …
- Brad Pitt plays a …
- The film **stars** Eva Green as a … / in the role of a …
- I thought the acting was terrible.

Talking about the people behind the film

- The film's director …
- It **is based on** real events / a real story / a novel by…
- The **screenplay** was by …

Talking about elements of a film

- The soundtrack was great.
- The ending was very good / a real surprise / very **predictable**.
- The best scene was when …

Write four positive things about a film that will help persuade a friend to go see it with you.

action-packed *voller Action* **(to) be based on sth.** [beɪst] *auf etwas beruhen* **classic** ['klæsɪk] *Klassiker* **fascinating** ['fæsɪneɪtɪŋ] *faszinierend* **heart-warming** *herzerwärmend* **imaginative** [ɪ'mædʒɪnətɪv] *fantasievoll* **predictable** [prɪ'dɪktəbl] *voraussehbar* **romcom** ['rɒmkɒm] *romantische Komödie* **sci-fi** *(infml:* **science fiction***)* ['saɪ faɪ] **screenplay** ['skriːnpleɪ] *Drehbuch* **(to) stand** *ausstehen* **(to) star** [stɑː] *in der Hauptrolle zeigen* **thought-provoking** [prə'vəʊkɪŋ] *zum Nachdenken anregend* **unbelievable** [ˌʌnbɪ'liːvəbl] *unglaublich* **violent** ['vaɪələnt] *gewalttätig*

 Illustrationen: Christian Bartz, Berlin

4 Presenting your opinion in a panel discussion

a) Match up the following phrases which appear frequently in panel discussions. There is more than one correct answer.

1 I agree
2 You can't
3 I think
4 In my opinion,
5 I don't think
6 As we have seen,

[ ]	we've got any new ideas.
[ ]	this is the best idea to proceed[1].
[1]	with what you're saying.
[ ]	just say that without giving an explanation.
[ ]	the problem isn't just going to go away.
[ ]	this needs to be done immediately.

b) What do you know about the *Great Pacific Garbage Patch*[2]? Comment on the following statements using sentence beginnings like in a). Write in your exercise book.

1 We don't need to care about a bit of rubbish in the water.

I disagree, because fish eat the plastic and we eat the fish.

2 Plastic isn't dangerous so there's no problem.
3 The sea is so huge it can take all that rubbish.
4 Countries throw radioactive waste in the sea, so what does a bit of rubbish matter?
5 Well, can't we just clean it up?
6 It won't affect me or my children, so I don't care.

c) You are a member of the local Association of Conservation[3] Volunteers, and you believe water pollution is becoming a huge problem. Prepare a two-minute introduction speech to a panel discussion stating your opinion and backing it up with facts.

Check: Speaking

a) Vergleiche deine Antworten mit den Lösungen auf Seite 80 im Workbook.
b) Schätze deine Antworten mit einem grünen oder roten Gesicht ein.

	☺	☹	
1 PRONUNCIATION Word stress Konntest du die Wörter richtig und ohne Probleme aussprechen?	○	○	→ 1
2 WORDS Defining words Konntest du die richtigen Wörter finden und umschreiben?	○	○	→ 2
3 USING ADVERBS Konntest du die unterstrichenen Wendungen in adverbiale Konstruktionen umwandeln?	○	○	→ 3, 4
4 Presenting your opinion in a panel discussion Konntest du vollständige Sätze bilden? Hast du verschiedene Redewendungen benutzt? Konntest du die Rede überzeugend präsentieren?	○	○	→ 5

c) Wenn du dich rot eingeschätzt hast, schau dir die rechte Spalte an. Die Nummern führen dich zu den passenden Übungen im Skills Training (S. 42–43). Dort kannst du gezielt Speaking trainieren.

[1]proceed [prə'siːd] *fortfahren* [2]patch [pætʃ] *Fleck* [3]conservation [ˌkɒnsə'veɪʃn] *Naturschutz*

1 PRONUNCIATION Word stress

22 Say the words and mark the stressed syllables. Then listen, check and say the words again.

1 analogy 2 application 3 compensate 4 electric 5 moderator 6 pilot

2 WORDS Improving your vocabulary

Identify the following words from the unit.

1 The process of improving something is known as ____________________.

2 Companies or people that have no money left are said to be ____________________.

3 Cancer treatments can leave your ____________________ system weak.

4 ____________________ products are grown without the use of artificial chemicals.

5 A ____________________ description is one which gives a lot of information in just a few words.

6 Topics which divide people are known as ____________________ issues.

7 ____________________ is the use of robots to do a job.

8 If you are not happy with a service you receive, it is your right to ____________________.

3 Speaking more naturally

a) Copy the table in your exercise book. Identify the following types of adverbs/adverbial phrases and write them in the right column.

after all · always · at first · calmly · carefully · constantly · even · for a few more years · in the garden · in the same place · later · of course · really · recently · regularly · right away · simply · still

Sentence adverbs	Adverbs of frequency	Adverbs of indefinite time	Adverbs of manner	Adverbs of place	Adverbs of time	Adverbs of degree

b) Rewrite the following phrases using the adverbs/adverbial phrases in brackets ( ). Use your exercise book.

1 We meet up to practise (in the same place/regularly).

We meet up regularly to practise in the same place.

2 We have to make sure we close the windows (always/carefully).

3 Our neighbours are complaining they can hear our music (constantly/in the garden).

4 We used to ignore them, but it has got worse (at first/recently).

5 They've started threatening to call the police if we don't stop (even/right away).

6 I told Mum I thought they were being rude, but she suggested we try talking to them (calmly/simply).

7 It's not going to be easy, but I'm going to do my best not to get annoyed when we go round to their house (later/of course/really).

TIP: Remember the **sequence** for adverbials in most cases:
- **Front position:** *sentence adverbs*
- **Mid-position:** *adverbs of frequency* and *indefinite time*
- **End position:** *adverbs of manner, place* and *time*
- **Before the word they refer to:** *adverbs of degree*

4 Becoming more environmentally friendly

In your exercise book, rewrite the sentences using adjectives/adverbial phrases instead of the underlined adverbs. Make any necessary changes. One example has already been done for you.

1 We should deal with environment issues logically.

We should deal with environment issues in a logical manner.

2 It would be much easier to save the planet if we behaved more consciously.

3 Worryingly, some people – including politicians – still believe that global warming isn't real.

4 But, recently, more and more people have started living in a more 'environmentally friendly' way.

5 They believe, for instance, that paying a little more for renewable electricity helps the environment effectively.

6 We need to tell people explicitly what they need to do to save the planet from further damage.

5 PANEL DISCUSSION Organizing what you say ➔ SF 17–19 (pp. 64–66)

Complete the table below with phrases you might hear during a panel discussion. Add your own phrases.

Although the lady makes a very good point … · As the lady mentioned … · *In my opinion …* · I think so too. · It often isn't as simple as that. · It's a known fact that … · Just a moment, please, to finish my point … · Personally, I believe … · So, to begin … · To open, I'd like to say … · We've already heard how … · You've already had your say.

Good ways to start	Presenting my position	Agreeing and disagreeing	Referring to what someone said	Reacting to what someone is saying	Reacting to interruptions
______	*In my opinion…*	______	______	______	______
______	______	______	______	______	______
______	______	______	______	______	______
______	______	______	______	______	______
______	______	______	______	______	______
______	______	______	______	______	______
______	______	______	______	______	______
______	______	______	______	______	______
______	______	______	______	______	______
______	______	______	______	______	______
______	______	______	______	______	______
______	______	______	______	______	______

1 Time to get moving? (Verb forms)

Read this blog article, looking carefully at the verb forms. There are some mistakes. Mark the mistakes and write the correct verb forms in your exercise book.

> **TIP:** Pay special attention to:
> - third-person singular 's'
> - simple/progressive forms
> - simple past/present perfect
> - *was/were*
> - questions/statements with *do/did*
> - the infinitive

Did you know that one of the most dangerous things we can do is lead a "sedentary lifestyle"? This mean a life with no – or not enough – regular physical activity. Sedentary people are sitting for most of the day, every day: in cars, on public transport, at work or school, at home or in pubs and restaurants. For a person who live in a rich country such as the UK or the USA, it is normal to spend over 70 % of the time you are awake sitting in a chair. How did this happened? From an evolutionary perspective, humans were designed to move all day long. In the past, this were necessary for us to survive as a species. But today, the way we live is quite different – even compared with the way people have lived 100 or even 50 years ago. Back then, most people didn't worked in an office or owned a car. Experts now believe that a sedentary lifestyle cause health problems such as type 2 diabetes and coronary heart disease. In 2017 a British study has found that British men spent the equivalent of 78 days sitting every year – and women 74 days. That doesn't sound good, did it? If you're not thinking that your lifestyle is sedentary, let me ask you this: how long you spend sitting every day? The answer could be surprising you. I haven't use to worry about my way of life at all, because I cycle to school. The problem is that my bike ride only takes ten minutes each way, which isn't enough. Luckily, we only have to change small things in our everyday routine to became healthier.

2 What is the future of work? (Verb tenses and modal verbs)

> could · should · needn't · can't

Complete this article from a school magazine with verbs in their correct forms and tenses. When you need a modal verb, choose the correct one from the box. You can use each modal verb only once.

Do you know what you (1) *are going to do* (do) when you leave school? The world of work (2) __________ (develop) very quickly at the moment. When our parents and grandparents (3) __________ (be) young, it was easier. Since then, things (4) __________ (change). New technology (5) __________ (make) some jobs unnecessary now. Experts believe that 40 % of jobs (6) __________ (modal verb) be lost to computers in the next 30 to 40 years! Already, we (7) __________ (see) engineers develop amazing things such as cars that drive themselves. We (8) __________ (modal verb) consider these things when we choose a job. However, we (9) __________ (modal verb) worry about all jobs disappearing in the future. Experts (10) __________ (agree) that many jobs (11) __________ (modal verb) be done by computers: social jobs such as teaching, creative jobs in the arts and sciences, and other jobs such as gardening probably (12) __________ (not disappear) in the future. In the 1930s, people (13) __________ (think) that new technology in mines and factories would have a terrible effect on the world of work, but it didn't. And I suppose new technology (14) __________ (create) jobs in the coming years as well. I, personally, don't know what I (15) __________ (study) yet, but I (16) __________ (feel) quite optimistic.

3 Test your knowledge: persuasion techniques and other devices

What devices have what function in a text? Next to each function, write the correct device from the box.

adverb · heading · italics · metaphor · personal pronoun *we* · personal pronoun *you* · ~~rhetorical question~~ · simile · statistics

1 says something in an emphatic way ___*rhetorical question*___

2 guides the reader ______

3 modifies a statement ______

4 shows that something is a book/song title ______

5 suggests that one thing is another ______

6 suggests that your argument is based on facts ______

7 makes the readers feel that you are talking to them directly ______

8 compares things using *like* or *as* ______

9 suggests you have something in common with the reader ______

4 Stephanie: a profile (Collocations: adverbs and adjectives as modifiers)

Complete the text with adverbs (e.g. really, not particularly, absolutely) and adjectives (e.g. big, huge) as modifiers.

Stephanie is my mother's sister. She's almost 13 years younger than my mother, which is a **f***airly*______ (1) big age gap. They didn't **r**______ (2) grow up together, but they get on **q**______ (3) well. Stephanie is the sort of person who values her family a **l**______ (4). She is always inviting my brother and me to stay with her, and when we were little she was a **b**______ (5) part of our life: she came to all our concerts, football matches and special events – and it was clear that she **a**______ (6) loved spending time with us. Stephanie lives alone, and she says she **d**______ (7) prefers it that way. She was married for a few years, but her marriage was **n**______ (8) **p**______ (9) happy, so she got divorced. Stephanie is a **h**______ (10) fan of dogs and has two at the moment. They came from a home for rescued dogs and were **e**______ (11) shy at first, but Stephanie has helped them to become more confident and now they're like **t**______ (12) different dogs. She is a **g**______ (13) fan of hiking and often takes the dogs with her. They come home covered in mud, and since she's not **v**______ (14) good at cleaning, her flat is often dirty, but we don't mind. We love her anyway.

5 A radio report (Present progressive: active and passive forms)

Complete the journalist's sentences with verbs from the box in the present progressive. Use the passive form if needed.

ask · film · ~~get~~ · not give · play · present · (now) take · wait

1 As we speak, the royal couple *is getting* ready to leave the plane.

2 The president ______________________ to meet them on the red carpet[1].

3 The prince and princess ______________________ by lots of cameras.

4 The prince ______________________ any flowers because he doesn't like them.

5 The princess ______________________ to the minister for science and technology.

6 A band ______________________ a traditional song for the couple.

7 The fans outside the airport ______________________ not to stand in the road.

8 The royal guests ______________________ to their first meeting.

6 Ideas for saving the planet from plastic (Verb tenses: active and passive forms)

Complete this article from a youth magazine with verbs in the correct forms and tenses, active and passive.

(1) ______________________ (you ever wish) that there were better alternatives to plastic bags? It is true that stronger shopping bags are better than single-use plastic bags, but some of them (2) ______________________ (still not consider) good for the environment. A couple of years ago, a young man in Indonesia (3) ______________________ (find) a great solution: bags made of cassava, a local vegetable. The bags are quite popular now and they (4) ______________________ (describe) as not being harmful to humans, animals or plants. The young man (5) ______________________ (show) that this was true in a video last year, by putting a bag into hot water and then drinking the mixture. For anyone who (6) ______________________ (ever feel) bored with coffee and tea, this could be a chance to try something different! For many years now, environmental organizations (7) ______________________ (tell) us about the dangers of plastic in our oceans. The fact that there are new non-plastic products on the market now suggests that a growing number of companies (8) ______________________ (start) to listen. A UK company (9) ______________________ (try) to fight the problem of plastic bottles with its new water "bubbles" made of a material that can be eaten. People from the company (10) ______________________ (test) them for a few months now. It is hoped that products like this (11) ______________________ (have) a positive influence on the plastic problem. However, experts expect that the positive influence (12) ______________________ (probably not be) enough to make people change their habits.

[1] carpet ['kɑːpɪt]

7 Identifying yourself online ➜ SF 17–18 (pp. 64–65)

Should everyone use their real name when taking part in online networks? Read the quotes and the questions below. Take notes in your exercise book. Then talk about the topic with a partner. You can record what you say. Talk to each other for about eight minutes altogether.

"I use my own name and photo online. I have nothing to hide, so what's the problem?"

"I never use my real name online. What if the websites I use were hacked and everyone could read what I'd written?"

"Some of the most interesting blogs I read are written under a false name. It lets the writers be more honest."

"Social networks don't give a true picture of people's lives. This creates a false identity."

"Bullies use false names so that they don't get caught."

"In some parts of the world, people have to use false names online if they want to start a political movement."

"I think it's good that we can choose to use a false name or a real name online."

"Online, you can be whoever you want to be."

a) Outline how you or your friends present yourselves on social media: do you use your real name or a false name? Do your profile photos show your face? Why (not)? How do your parents or other adults you know present themselves on social media?

b) Explain the advantages and disadvantages of using a false name online. For example, how might false names protect people? How might false names influence the way people behave online?

c) Reflect on the question of how social media might change if a new law made everyone use their real name when taking part in online networks. Would you support this law? Why (not)?

d) Some people say that using a false name makes them feel safer online. Discuss other ways to stay safe online. You could consider passwords, sharing personal information, posting party invitations, etc. What tips would you give to younger students at your school? Try to sound polite even if you have different points of view. You can use some of the following expressions:

- **Giving reasons for your opinion:**
  Let me explain why … In my opinion, … This is how I feel …
- **Supporting your argument with examples:**
  I'll give you an example of what I mean … Another thing, …
- **Saying that you disagree:**
  But I feel very strongly that … That's not how I see it … I'm not sure I share your view …
- **Interrupting your partner:**
  Sorry, but could I just say something?
- **Answering when your partner interrupts:**
  Yes, of course. Go ahead, please …
- **Pointing out shared views:**
  So we both agree that …
- **Stating your conclusions:**
  To sum up, we could say that … On a few points, I think we'll have to agree to differ …

8 How to be happy: do hunter-gatherer[1] tribes hold the key? ➜ SF 1–2 (p. 56)

a) Reading for gist: skim the text. Which sentence summarizes the text? Circle A, B or C.

A Living in the present makes us happier, but people in the West have lost sight of this.

B Mobile phones are now the main cause of problems in the Western world.

C Hunter-gatherer tribes are happier because they don't worry about money.

As part of our *Meet the Researcher* series, we're presenting our university's staff and their research interests. This week, Dr Rebecca Selwyn reveals how tribal societies may hold the key to human happiness.

I majored in Anthropology and have worked at the university for ten years. During this time, I also lived with hunter-gatherer tribes in very remote parts of Malaysia and on the Pacific Northwest Coast to study how they live. I came back to the US regularly to lecture at the university. Moving between the two extremes of small villages and large, busy US cities for so many years has given me what I believe to be a different perspective on one of the most fundamental things in life: happiness. Observing these tribal societies and seeing how happy their members are compared with people in the Western world has shown me that we Westerners absolutely do not understand the true meaning of life. We are driven by the need to improve everything, and we see humankind as always moving towards a state of perfection. We are always focused on the future and we wrongly think that increasing our productivity by working harder and using more and more new technologies will finally lead us to some kind of paradise where everything is perfect.

I think people in the West are on the wrong path, but it's not really our fault: this idealization of productivity and hard work is deeply rooted in our culture. It dates back to the Industrial Revolution when people wanted everything to work faster and better and – in the US – it is also a product of the American dream. We should have started to notice by now, though, that even with all the advances in technology, we are not enjoying more free time. The hunter-gatherer tribes that I lived with know better. They spend just 15 to 20 hours a week getting food and another 10 to 15 hours on domestic work. The rest of the time, they are free to do what they want. Anthropologists believe that life was like this for most of the history of humanity. Looking backward or forward through time is a relatively recent thing. "My tribes", for example, do not have much of a sense of history, and details about their ancestors are of little interest to them. They see no need to set goals, either. Of course, they notice the seasons changing, but that is all.

Part of my research now focuses on what we can learn from hunter-gatherer tribes about being happy. Mindfulness – living in the present – is key. It can be achieved in different ways, and meditation is a popular one today. But it's ironic and a little sad that people in the West need apps to clear their mind when the reason they need to clear their mind in the first place is that they use too many apps! I think there are better ways to improve our relationship with time than to use cell phones or tablets for meditation. We just need to get into a "flow state". This is when you are so interested in what you are doing that you forget all about the passing of time. The tribes I have lived with get into this state naturally, simply by doing an activity that brings them joy. In the Western world, we can achieve flow by taking away all distractions – especially electronic devices – and letting ourselves concentrate on something fun: writing a story, practicing a sport, playing chess …

Achieving a flow state is a good start, but in the West, we really need to change our whole idea that things will always be better in the future. There's a quotation I like by the German inventor Frederick Koenig. Even though he was a man of the Industrial Revolution, it sums up what our attitude should be today. It goes something like this: "being happy doesn't come from getting something you don't have, but from realizing what you do have." That is what differentiates us from hunter-gatherer tribes – they just enjoy what they have instead of trying to get something better.

[1] gatherer ['gæðərə] *Sammler/in*

b) **Reading for detail:** Are the statements below true or false?
Give the number of the line(s) where you found the answer.

1 Dr Selwyn had a job at a university in Malaysia for ten years. F ll. 8–12

2 She believes that life is not about making things better.

3 People in the West have the right idea about life, although they need a little help.

4 Hunter-gatherers have a lot of time to relax, even though they have to work to find food.

5 The tribes that Dr Selwyn studied do not consider the past to be important.

6 She recommends using special mobile phone apps to achieve focus and flow.

7 Moving your body is the only way to achieve a flow state.

8 The inventor Koenig had the right idea about how to enjoy life.

c) Summarize how hunter-gatherer tribes and people in the Western world think about time. Write in your exercise book.

d) Examine the writer's attitude towards the way in which people in the Western world live. Write in your exercise book.

e) Reflect on the quotation "being happy doesn't come from getting something you don't have, but from realizing what you do have." What does it mean, and do you agree with it? What kind of things and situations make people happy? Write in your exercise book.

I think the meaning of the quotation is this: if you ... Although I agree with the quotation, I believe that it is too ... I don't agree with the quotation because ...
The things that make people happy are ...

9 Does what you own actually own you?

Look at the cartoon on the right and do the tasks below.
You should talk for at least three minutes altogether.
Make notes. You can record what you say.

a) Describe the cartoon and analyse it.

b) Interpret the message of the cartoon.
What does it say about modern life?

c) Comment on the cartoon's message.
Do you agree with it? What would you recommend doing?
Do you agree with the idea that "what you own actually owns you"?

10 Talking about identity and expression

Read the quotation and do the tasks a)–c). Make notes. You can record what you say. You should talk for at least three minutes altogether.

a) In your own words, state the author's message.

b) Illustrate the advantages and disadvantages of "being who you are" as a young person.

c) Discuss how social media can make it easier or more difficult for young people to be themselves.

"Be who you are and say what you feel, because those who mind don't matter and those who matter don't mind."

Dr Seuss, US author, 1904–1991

11 Creating a feeling of belonging at school ➔ SF 3–6 (pp. 56–58), 13–15 (pp. 62–64)

a) Your school receives the email below. Read the email and do the following tasks.

Hello,

We're a group of students from the UK, and we're writing to schools around Europe to ask for help. We're trying to change the rule about wearing a uniform at our school, because we don't believe uniforms help us to learn. However, our head teacher says that we must keep the uniform because it creates a feeling of belonging and helps students to identify with the school.

We know that there are schools all over Europe that don't have uniforms – so there must be other ways to create these positive feelings at school. Could you tell us what you think about uniforms and rules about clothes – and how these things do or don't help you feel part of your school? What other things can help you feel like you belong? We'll use your feedback for our project.

Thank you!
Riverview Comprehensive Students' Council

b) In your exercise book, reply to the email.
- Describe what the rules are for clothes and appearance at your school.
- Illustrate how a uniform could create a feeling of belonging at school (or in a school sports team or other group). Do you think just having a uniform would be enough to create this feeling? Why (not)?
- Reflect on other things that could help students to identify with their school. What could students, teachers and parents do to help? Write 180–250 words.

Find a suitable introduction and conclusion for your text.

Some ideas to think about:

- Can a school uniform prevent bullying/pressure to look trendy and make school a nicer place?
- Can wearing a uniform (at school or in a sports team, choir, etc.) make you feel proud? Can it influence the way you behave?
- If everyone dresses the same in a team or group, does it help them feel that they belong?
- Do teachers who spend a lot of time checking students' uniforms have less time for more important tasks?
- Can concerts, groups, clubs, trips, a school magazine or shared activities or experiences help students identify with the school? What about making the school a nice place to be (e.g. looking after the school buildings and environment, or having a culture of kindness)?

12 Local currencies ➔ SF 22–24 (p. 68)

You are doing a group project at school about people's hometowns and their identity. You find an English radio programme about local currencies in the UK.

a) 23 Listen and take notes on what local currencies are, how they work and how they can help people identify more strongly with where they live. If you need help, look at p. 54.

b) In your exercise book, write a summary of the relevant information in German for your project group. Write 120–150 words.

13 Tips for reducing rubbish ➔ SF 11 (p. 61) • SF 22–24 (p. 68)

a) Your American friend Caleb has to write a report for school about how people can reduce the amount of rubbish they produce.
He has found an interesting article on a German website, but he doesn't understand everything.
Read the article and mark the relevant sentences/parts.

„Zero Waste": Gut leben und gleichzeitig Abfall vermeiden

Anhänger der „Zero-Waste"-Bewegung versuchen, keinen Müll zu produzieren, der auf der Deponie landet. Wie dies in der Großstadt geschehen kann, erzählt die 17-jährige Mathilda aus Berlin.

Meine Eltern waren schon immer umweltbewusst. Plastiktüten, Einwegstrohhalme und unnötige Werbeartikel wie Kugelschreiber haben wir immer vermieden. Vor fünf Jahren ist meine Mutter über einen Blog gestolpert, der unser Leben verändert hat. Er wurde von einer Frau in den USA geführt, die zu Hause überhaupt keinen Abfall produzierte, der nicht recycelt oder kompostiert werden kann. Meine Eltern fanden die Idee toll und wollten sofort nach deren Prinzipien leben. Mein Bruder und ich waren am Anfang eher skeptisch. Wir hatten aber keine andere Wahl!

Meine Eltern mussten zuerst viel recherchieren. Nach und nach haben wir es dann geschafft, immer weniger Müll zu produzieren. Es ist eigentlich nicht so schwer. Man muss sich nur ein wenig umstellen. Der wichtigste Schritt war, in „Unverpackt-Läden" einzukaufen, um Verpackungsmüll zu vermeiden. Wenn wir einkaufen gehen, bringen wir immer abfüllbare Behälter mit. Wir kaufen auch regelmäßig bei Bauernhöfen, beim Bäcker, im Bioladen und auf dem Wochenmarkt ein, weil auch dort lose Waren angeboten werden. Es ist toll, weil wir nur so viel einkaufen, wie wir wirklich brauchen, das spart auch Geld. Man kann auch viele Produkte selber machen, um Plastikmüll zu vermeiden. Meine Mutter macht zum Beispiel Shampoo aus Avocadokernen und wir mischen uns Zahnpulver aus Birkenzucker (in der Apotheke erhältlich) und Natron. Da die meisten Plastikzahnbürsten nicht recyclebar sind, kaufen wir kompostierbare Bambus-Zahnbürsten. Wir verwenden Kaffeesatz in der Dusche als Körperpflege. Ich habe auch vor Kurzem gelernt, wie man Make-up selbst erstellt. Ich mache auch gern Kerzen aus Kerzenresten.

Obwohl wir in einer Wohnung im dritten Stock wohnen, kompostieren wir viele Reste. Wir haben im Gemeinschaftsgarten einen Wurmkomposter und verwenden unseren kompostierten Müll für Blumen und Gemüsebeete. Wer Gemüse selbst anbaut, spart viel Müll. Auf den Fensterbrettern in unserer Wohnung stehen kleine Töpfe mit Kräutern. Wichtig ist, dass wir kaum Lebensmittel verschwenden, auch wenn die Essensreste kompostierbar sind. Jeden Sonntag planen meine Eltern, was sie in der kommenden Woche kochen wollen. Natürlich kann es trotzdem Speisereste geben. In dem Fall bereiten wir daraus andere Mahlzeiten, wie z.B. eine Suppe, zu. Aus Obstresten kann man ein leckeres Müsli kreieren. (Mein Lieblingstipp? Bananenschalen zum Schuheputzen. Meine Freunde fanden das total abgefahren – bis sie es ausprobierten.) Eine gute Vorbereitung ist ebenfalls unerlässlich, wenn man draußen isst. Wir haben immer Stoffservietten, Trinkflaschen und Reisebesteck dabei.

Die Leute fragen mich oft, ob ich ein Handy bzw. einen Fernseher habe. Viele denken, wir dürfen keine Elektrogeräte benutzen. Das stimmt nicht! Handys sind ein tolles Mittel, um Papier zu vermeiden. Wenn ich unterwegs bin, fotografiere ich Flyer oder Flugblätter, damit ich sie nicht mitnehmen muss. Das ist nur ein Beispiel. Wir benutzen Elektrogeräte so lange wie möglich und lassen sie reparieren, bis sie nicht mehr zu retten sind. Erst dann werden sie fachgerecht entsorgt.

Ich bin es mittlerweile gewohnt, „abfallfrei" zu leben. Das möchte ich gern fortsetzen, weil es einfach schön ist, zu wissen, dass man etwas für die Umwelt tut.

b) Write an email to Caleb summarizing the ideas about reducing rubbish that you have read about in the article in a). Write 150–200 words.

14 What's for dinner? → SF 27 (p. 70)

24 In the USA, the way people eat is changing. In this radio programme, Sonari Glinton interviews people about how Americans' dinner habits have developed in recent years.
You will have six minutes to read the tasks. Then you will listen to the recording.
After that, you will have three minutes to do the tasks. Then you will listen to the recording again.
Finally, you will have another three minutes to complete the tasks.
You may write while you are listening. If you need help, look at p. 55.

a) Are the statements below true or false? Write *T* or *F* in the box.

1 It was harder to answer the question "What's for dinner?" 30 years ago than it is today.

2 Sonari Glinton interviews his mother because she has always wanted to be on the radio.

3 As a child, Sonari Glinton was only allowed to eat fast food at weekends.

4 Sonari Glinton's mother often makes soup or salad for dinner.

b) Tick (✓) the correct answer. Only one answer is correct.

A groceraunt is
1 a restaurant that will bring your dinner to your home.
2 a restaurant where staff cook the food at your table.
3 a store selling meals that have already been prepared.
4 a salad bar.

c) Complete the sentences with one to five words.

Bonnie Riggs has not been cooking as much because ______.

As she drives home from work, she will pass ______ places offering high-quality, ______ food.

d) Are the statements below true or false? Write *T* or *F* in the box.

1 Elliott Silver and Noah Ellis own the *Red Medicine* restaurant. ☐

2 A meal at *Picnic LA* costs 15 dollars. ☐

3 At *Picnic LA*, six workers are needed for 150 guests. ☐

4 Being a new kind of restaurant, *Picnic LA* doesn't have any competition yet. ☐

e) Complete the sentence.

Blue Apron is an online service that brings you ______________________________:

everything you need to ______________________________.

f) Tick (✓) the correct answer. Only one answer is correct.

Matt Salzberg says one problem people have with cooking is

1 it costs a lot of money. ☐

2 TV shows make it look more fun than it is. ☐

3 it's boring. ☐

4 nobody has the time to do it. ☐

g) Which summary of the radio programme is correct? Circle A, B or C.

A If you ask, "What's for dinner?", the answer is different to what it was 30 years ago. People have more choices today, and they spend a lot more money on healthy food.

B Most people in West Hollywood don't plan what they are going to have for dinner because they don't have time to cook. There is a gap in the market for companies that make cooking easier.

C The question "What's for dinner?" is not difficult to answer. There are many new kinds of places to eat – and for those who want to cook, new services make it easier.

12 Local currencies

23 If you need help to understand the text, you may read the transcript while you are listening.

Announcer:
Hello, and welcome to *The Money in Your Pocket* Podcast. This week's topic is local currencies. Here to talk about them is our money reporter, Olly Bradshaw.

Olly:
If you're planning a trip to Liverpool any time soon, there are a few things you'll need: a camera to capture all the great sights, an umbrella in case it rains ... and the Liverpool pound. OK, so the last one isn't compulsory, but the Liverpool pound has really taken the city by storm since it was launched in 2016. And it's just one of several local currencies being used around the UK.

So, what exactly is a local currency? Well, it's quite simple. It's a currency that can only be spent in a certain city with businesses that have specifically joined the project. It doesn't replace the official currency, but it can be used as an alternative way to pay for goods and services at shops, cafes, restaurants and other businesses.

The idea of local currencies isn't new, but these schemes have experienced a renaissance in recent years because of globalization. Many people want their money to go to local businesses instead of huge international companies.

You might be wondering how local currencies work. Well, you can't just go and get the Liverpool pound from the bank, because it's a virtual currency, a digital currency. What you have to do, is download the currency app to your smartphone, and then you can move money from your real bank account to your Liverpool pound account. Then, you can use your smartphone to pay in any shop or business that is a member. It's like having a digital wallet. Most of the other local currencies in the UK work in the same way. Some of them have paper money – such as the systems in Brixton and Bristol – but these currencies are also digital and can be used on smartphones.

So far, so easy. But do local currencies really make a difference? Absolutely. If a local currency is only accepted in the local community, it encourages people to buy things from local shops. So, it helps local businesses, making the city richer.

But, just as importantly, local currencies also help people to feel part of a city. Think about it: if you use a local currency, you will discover new, local shops and cafés, and you will probably go there regularly because they accept this new payment system. In this way, you make new friends, because you see the same people at the cafes and shops every time. The Liverpool pound can make a person from Liverpool feel more connected to their city because of its personal touch – and this works for people who have lived there all their lives, or people who have just moved there. So, the local currency actually strengthens people's identity as a citizen or a resident of Liverpool or Brixton, or Bristol.

The people who started these schemes understand this, and they even advertise the currencies as a way to get to know your city better and to show that you love the city and support the local community. It's like belonging to a special club for people from your city.

Another way that local currencies help people identify with their city is through their images. I mentioned that some of the local currencies have a paper version as well as a digital version. Bristol Pound notes feature symbols of local pride and famous people who came from Bristol and achieved great things. Brixton's ten-pound note features an image of David Bowie, who was born in that part of London. The money reminds people to be proud of their city when they use it.

What are the disadvantages of local currencies? Well, there aren't many, but as they are not legal tender, people might not get their money back from their account if the scheme fails. The digital system also excludes people without smartphones. Perhaps an extra currency makes shopping more complicated too. But so far, the people of Liverpool, Brixton and Bristol don't seem to have had many problems.

14 What's for dinner?

24 If you need help to understand the text, you may read the transcript while you are listening.

Audie Cornish: Here in Washington, it's getting late in the day. Do you know what you're having for dinner? According to the food data company *Food Genius*, as many as 80 percent of you don't. Answering that question is a growing business. In collaboration with Youth Radio, NPR's Sonari Glinton asked the age-old question, what's for dinner?
Sonari Glinton: Let's face it. Knowing what you're going to have for dinner ahead of time isn't nearly as important as it used to be. Increasingly, we're calling audibles[1]. I'm standing in the parking lot at the new Shake Shack in West Hollywood, and it's just one of hundreds of choices I have in this neighborhood. Now, answering the question what's for dinner, it's pretty easy here. And that's true for a good part of the US. But that wasn't the case, say, I don't know, 30 years ago.
Dorothy Glinton: I knew what we were going to eat when I come out the grocery store on a Saturday all week.
Sonari Glinton: That's my mama.
Dorothy Glinton: I am Dorothy Glinton. I'm Sonari Glinton's mother.
Sonari Glinton: Look, once in a career you can put your own mom on the radio. And I'm doing it now because if there ever was an expert in putting food on the table, I'm telling you, it's Dorothy Glinton.
Dorothy Glinton: And cooking wasn't a big deal for me. And it wasn't – it was easy stuff. Put a pot roast in the oven while we did homework at night so the next day all I had to do was heat it up. And I always knew what I was going to cook. I didn't come in running.
Sonari Glinton: Now, back then, I never ate fast food because I grew up with a mom who wouldn't allow it. Now, though, even she eats out on weeknights.
Dorothy Glinton: But I don't go to a restaurant when I – you know, in the evening. I do most of my eating in a grocery store now, picking up a hot soup, going to a salad bar.
Bonnie Riggs: We're calling that groceraunt.
Sonari Glinton: That's Bonnie Riggs. She's a restaurant industry analyst.
Bonnie Riggs: A groceraunt is a grocery store like a Mariano's that offers prepared meals for immediate consumption.
Sonari Glinton: Riggs says grocery stores offering prepared meals are just one example. The point is how we answer that question, what's for dinner, it's changing.
Bonnie Riggs: I don't know if I'm going out to dinner or if I'm going to go home and cook. And I just have not been cooking as much lately as I have historically.
Sonari Glinton: Well, that's because she doesn't have to. As she drives home from work, Riggs will pass hundreds of places offering high-quality, fresh food at reasonable prices – grocery stores, food trucks, takeout, drive-thrus. Even *Uber* delivers food. And old restaurant concepts, like the automat and the cafeteria, are making a comeback. I'm at *Picnic LA* with Elliott Silver and Noah Ellis and – the two restaurant guys used to own a fancy pants restaurant in Beverly Hills. What was the name of it?
Elliot Silver: *Red Medicine*.
Sonari Glinton: What made you go from wanting to, like, open a high-end restaurant to opening what is a – what I have to – no offense – I have to call a high-end cafeteria?
Elliot Silver: Same reason we opened *Red Medicine*. We wanted to open a restaurant we wanted to eat at.
Sonari Glinton: For 15 bucks at *Picnic LA* in Culver City, you can get an entree like poached salmon and two sides. Think cafeteria but really nice – local, organic and a little hipster.
Noah Ellis: So we try to display the produce, right? We've got Weiser Farm potatoes, par-cooked, the little gems just came in, the asparagus from Zuckerman's, fennel from JF Organics.
Sonari Glinton: One reason Silver and Ellis did not start another full-service restaurant is labor costs. The minimum wage is going up. *Picnic LA* might serve, say, 150 people tonight. They will need just six employees to do that.
Noah Ellis: We were eating in sort of higher end restaurants and just wanted to make it more accessible.
Sonari Glinton: Now, *Picnic LA* is a new type of restaurant that didn't exist a few years ago. But it too faces competition.
Matt Salzberg: My name is Matt Salzberg, and I am a co-founder and CEO of *Blue Apron*.
Sonari Glinton: *Blue Apron* is an online service that delivers the ingredients and recipes, everything you need to make your dinner.
Matt Salzberg: Interest in food is higher than it's ever been, but culinary skills are ironically lower than they've ever been.
Sonari Glinton: The *Food Channel*, Martha Stewart and even Rachael Ray have helped give us more knowledge about food and culinary culture. But our schedules are keeping us from practicing our cooking skills in our own kitchens.
Matt Salzberg: We like to cook but we found it expensive. We found it difficult to assemble ingredients. And we found it inaccessible.
Sonari Glinton: *Blue Apron* isn't the only new food delivery service. *GrubHub*, *AmazonFresh*, even *Uber* is getting in on the dinner game says Bonnie Riggs.

[1] call an audible [ˈɔːdəbl] *eine Entscheidung in letzter Minute treffen (aus dem Football)*

SF 1 Skimming and scanning ➜ *SB (p. 105)*

Skimming *(reading for gist)* und **Scanning** *(reading for specific information)* sind Lesetechniken, die viel Zeit sparen, v. a. beim Lesen von langen Texten.

Skimming

Skimming hilft, schnell zu sehen, ob ein Text für deinen Zweck geeignet ist.

Step 1: Sieh dir diese Textteile an, um zu sehen, worum es im Text geht:
- Überschrift und Unterüberschriften
- Bilder und Bildunterschriften
- den ersten Satz jedes Absatzes – dieser Satz ist meist der *topic sentence*, der die Hauptidee des Absatzes beinhaltet
- den letzten Absatz des Textes, der oft eine Zusammenfassung des Textes enthält

Step 2: Fasse für dich selbst den Text in ein paar Worten zusammen. Wenn dir das ohne Probleme gelingt, dann weißt du, um was es in dem Text geht – und dass dein Skimming erfolgreich war.

> **TIPP:** Mach dir um unbekannten Wortschatz erstmal keine Gedanken – dafür ist Zeit, wenn du feststellst, dass der Text für dich geeignet ist.

Scanning

Scanning hilft, in einem Text schnell nach bestimmten Informationen zu suchen.

Step 1: Überlege dir *keywords*. Suchst du z. B. die Öffnungszeiten eines Museums, könnten das Wörter sein wie *open*, *hours* oder *days*.

Step 2: Überfliege den Text und suche nach den *keywords*. Du kannst dabei mit dem Finger in einer „S-Form" durch den Text gehen.

Step 3: Lies die Textstelle, die dein *keyword* enthält, um zu sehen, ob sie die gewünschten Informationen enthält. Wenn nicht, scanne weiter.

> **TIPP:** Wenn du mit Texten **im Internet** arbeitest, kann dein Browser dir viel Arbeit abnehmen.
> Mit **Strg+F (Cmd+F** am Mac) kannst du nach deinen *keywords* suchen und nur die Textstellen lesen, in denen ein *keyword* markiert ist.

SF 2 Marking up a text ➜ *SB (p. 105)*

Auf Kopien von Texten kannst du Informationen markieren, um sie einfacher wiederzufinden, z. B. wenn du eine Zusammenfassung schreiben sollst.

Step 1: Lies die Aufgabe genau und überlege, welche Informationen du zur Beantwortung brauchst. Behalte dies beim Lesen des Textes im Kopf.

Step 2: Markiere nur Informationen, die wichtig sind (z. B. durch Unterstreichen, Einkreisen oder Markieren mit einem Textmarker). Oft reicht es, nur ein oder zwei Wörter in einem Satz zu markieren.

Step 3: Mach dir kurze Notizen am Rand – z. B. kurze Überschriften oder Stichwörter –, die den Inhalt kurz zusammenfassen. (➜ *SF 39*)

> **TIPP:**
> 1. Verwende unterschiedliche Farben für unterschiedliche Aufgaben/Fragestellungen.
> 2. Markiere wirklich nur Stichwörter, sonst wird es unübersichtlich.

Fifty years ago today, Rudy Lombard, who is black, and his friend Lanny Goldfinch, who is white, walked into a diner in downtown New Orleans. With two other black friends, they took seats at a whites-only counter. Immediately they were asked to leave. They didn't. Instead they sat

Many of those who took part were students, both white and black. Through their protests, they put themselves in great danger. People were arrested, beaten up and murdered. Some spent time in prison. Some lost their jobs

up and finally, after two years, th

SF 3 The stages of writing ➜ *SB (p. 106)*

Planungsphase

Step 1: Plane ausreichend Zeit ein und denke über folgende Fragen nach:
- Über welches Thema willst du schreiben?
- Was sollst du tun (beschreiben, erläutern, zusammenfassen …)?
- Welche Dinge musst du für den geforderten Text beachten?

Step 2: Dann solltest du
- alle nötigen Informationen für dein Thema **recherchieren**, (➜ *SF 30*)
- Ideen/Argumente sammeln und sortieren
- und eine Gliederung (**Outline**) für den Text (z. B. einen Bericht) machen. (➜ *SF 6*)

Entwurfsphase

Jetzt schreibe deinen ersten Entwurf:

- Füge deiner Outline **linking words** (➔ *SF 5*) und **topic sentences** hinzu (➔ *SF 4*).
- Beginne für jede neue Idee einen neuen Absatz.
- Führe deine Ideen aus und gib Beispiele (wenn das die Textsorte erfordert).
- Denk über das Ende deines Textes nach. Wenn du weißt, wie dein Text endet, ist es leichter, eine gute Einleitung zu schreiben, die darauf hinführt. (➔ *SF 4*)

Überarbeitungsphase

Wenn der Entwurf fertig ist, bist du mit deiner Arbeit am Text leider noch nicht durch – jetzt beginnt die Überarbeitung. Am besten ist es, wenn du oder jemand anderes deinen Text liest. Wenn du die Zeit hast, hilft es den Text mehrmals zu lesen, jedes Mal mit einem anderen Schwerpunkt:

- Liest sich der Text gut? Ist er logisch aufgebaut? Hat er eine **gute Struktur**? (➔ *SF 4*)
- Prüfe die **sprachlichen Aspekte** deines Textes: Grammatik, Rechtschreibung, Zeichensetzung, Ausdruck, *linking words, time markers*, etc. (➔ *SF 5, SF 14*)
- Schreibe deinen Text noch einmal ab. Verbessere alles, was im ersten Entwurf noch nicht ganz gepasst hat. Wenn du **Feedback** von jemand anderem bekommen hast, sieh es dir genau an und entscheide dann, was davon du für deinen Text übernehmen möchtest. (➔ *SF 29*)

TIPP: Mehr Informationen zum Verfassen guter Texte findest du auch in den folgenden Abschnitten:

- **SF 4:** Structuring texts
- **SF 5:** Writing good sentences
- **SF 6:** Making an outline
- **SF 7:** Writing an argumentative essay
- **SF 8:** Writing an article
- **SF 9:** Writing an opinion piece/ a comment
- **SF 10:** Writing a report
- **SF 11:** Writing a summary
- **SF 12:** Writing a review
- **SF 13:** Writing a formal letter or email
- **SF 14:** Revising texts
- **SF 15:** Revising and improving electronic tests
- **SF 30:** Finding information online

SF 4 Structuring texts ➔ *SB (p. 107)*

Struktur

Ein guter Text besteht in der Regel aus drei Teilen:

- **Einleitung** (*introduction*):
  Hier steht, worum es in dem Text geht. An dieser Stelle kann auch ein Problem genannt werden, das in dem Text erörtert werden soll.
- **Hauptteil** (*main body*):
  Dieser Teil ist in mehrere Absätze gegliedert und präsentiert die Details (Fakten, Beispiele etc.) zu deinem Thema.
- **Schluss** (*conclusion*):
  Hier gibst du deinem Text ein passendes Ende.

My Trip to Wales

Last summer I wanted to go to Wales because I like the mountains.

First I had to find some information on Wales. So I went to the library and looked for books about Wales. I found a book with some interesting information on hiking tours and I also found a camping guide for Wales. I went home with three books under my arm.

At home I started to plan for my trip. I read all the books and took notes on hiking trails, the weather and the equipment I would need for camping and hiking. After a few days I knew where I wanted to go and what I wanted to do there.

I did not want to go to Wales alone, so I had to find someone to go with me. I called most of my friends and told them about my plan. Some of them did not want to go hiking and others had no money for the trip. But my friend Judith agreed to go with me. We decided to go in late August.

Judith and I spent two lovely weeks in Wales. We went to Snowdonia and enjoyed the fantastic mountains. We stayed in a lovely bed and breakfast and met lots of really nice people. Before we went home we spent two very interesting days in Cardiff.

This was one of the best summer holidays I ever had. Go to Wales – it's fantastic!

Absätze

Längere Texte sind einfacher zu lesen und schneller zu verstehen, wenn sie in Absätze eingeteilt sind. Dabei solltest du folgende Dinge beachten:

- Fange für neue Aspekte einen neuen Absatz an.
- Beginne mit einem interessanten *topic sentence*.
- Beende deinen Text im letzten Absatz mit einer Zusammenfassung oder etwas Persönlichem.

Einleitungssätze

Jeder Absatz sollte mit einem Einleitungssatz beginnen.
Dieser *topic sentence* beschreibt, worum es in dem Absatz geht. Wichtige Dinge, die du in einem *topic sentence* ansprechen kannst, sind z. B.

- **Orte:** *My trip to Berlin was exciting.*
- **Personen:** *The Beatles are a famous band.*
- **Aktivitäten:** *Lots of people ride their bike every day.*

SF 5 Writing good sentences ➔ *SB (pp. 107–108)*

Adjektive

Verwende Adjektive, wenn du Dinge, Orte und Menschen näher beschreiben möchtest:

- *a **bright** face*
- *a **fantastic** trip*

Stell aber sicher, dass du die Adjektive **good**, **bad** und **nice** nicht zu häufig einsetzt. Ersetze sie durch andere Adjektive mit einer ähnlichen bzw. genaueren Bedeutung:

- *a **nice** teacher: a **friendly** teacher, a **helpful** teacher, …*
- *a **good** book: an **interesting** book, a **funny** book, …*

Adverbien

Verwende Adverbien, um Handlungen näher zu beschreiben:

- *They walked home **slowly**.*
- *She talked **quietly**.*

Verwende Ausdrücke wie **really**, **very**, **a bit** etc., um Aussagen zu verdeutlichen oder zu verstärken:

- *It was a **really** sad story.*
- *The houses are **very** high.*

Konjunktionen

Konjunktionen wie **and**, **but** oder **because** geben deinen Sätzen eine klare, gut nachvollziehbare Struktur:

- *We went to the London Eye, but it was **very** expensive.*

Relativsätze

Relativsätze verbinden Sätze oder geben mehr Informationen zu einer Sache oder einer Person:

- *This is the shop **which** sells the best ice cream in Berlin.*

Zeitangaben

Time markers/adverbiale Bestimmungen der Zeit helfen dem Leser, sich in einem Text oder einer Geschichte zeitlich zurechtzufinden. Verwende *time markers*, um …

- die **Reihenfolge von Ereignissen** zu verdeutlichen:
  at first, next, finally, …
- zu zeigen, **wie viel Zeit** zwischen einzelnen Ereignissen vergeht:
  for half an hour, just two minutes later, …
- zu verdeutlichen, **wie langsam oder schnell** etwas passiert:
  immediately, it took hours, faster than I could look, …
- zu sagen, wenn etwas **zeitgleich** passiert:
  while I was waiting, during the lesson, as we came round the corner, …
- die **Ereignisse eines Textes/einer Geschichte** zeitlich einzuordnen:
  two summers ago, last Halloween, on my way home from school yesterday, …

SF 6 Making an outline ➔ *SB (p. 108)*

Jede Art von Text profitiert davon, wenn du dir vorab überlegst, was du in welcher Reihenfolge schreiben willst.

- Wenn du einen Bericht schreiben sollst (➔ *SF 10*), kann es helfen, die wichtigsten Punkte schon in der **Gliederung** zu berücksichtigen: eine gute **Struktur** und die Beantwortung der ***wh*-Fragen**.
- Bei einer Zusammenfassung (➔ *SF 11*) kannst du hier die wichtigsten Punkte festhalten.
- Für eine Erörterung (➔ *SF 7*), einen Kommentar (➔ *SF 9*) oder einen Artikel (➔ *SF 8*) kannst du in deiner Outline schon die Argumente sortieren, die du im Text bringen möchtest.

Damit leistest du schon eine Menge Vorarbeit und erleichterst dir das Schreiben.

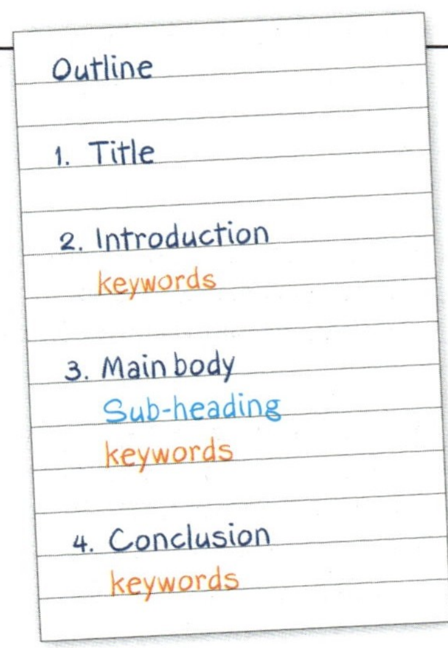

SF 7 Writing an argumentative essay ➔ *SB (p. 109)*

Planungsphase

Step 1: Lies die Aufgabe sorgfältig durch.

Step 2: Sammle Ideen und mache erste Notizen.
Schreibe alle Argumente pro *und* contra auf, die dir einfallen.

Step 3: Ordne deine Argumente, z. B. in Form einer Outline. (➔ *SF 6*)
Hebe das Argument hervor, das deine Position am besten unterstreicht – damit solltest du deinen Hauptteil beenden, denn das merken sich die Leser am ehesten.

Schreibphase

Step 1: Schreibe deine Einleitung: sage kurz, um welches Thema es geht, ohne deine eigene Meinung dazu zu äußern.

Step 2: Im Hauptteil präsentierst du die Argumente, die du dir überlegt hast.
Dabei helfen folgende Redemittel:

- **Presenting arguments:** *One of the main reasons why … / It is often said that … / Some people think … / In addition to these points …*
- **Ordering arguments:** *In the first place, … / Firstly,/Secondly,/Thirdly, … / Finally, … / First of all …*
- **Contrasting arguments:** *On the one hand – on the other hand / Contrary to what most people believe, … / While/Although …*
- **Giving examples:** *For example, … / This is clear because …*

Step 3: Am Schluss fasst du deine Argumente nochmal kurz zusammen und erklärst deine Schlussfolgerung:

- **Summing up arguments:** *To sum up, … / In conclusion, … / All in all, … / I would like to finish by pointing out again that …*
- **Explaining your conclusion:** *After looking at both sides of the argument, … / Although I understand the other side of the argument, I still think … / Personally, I believe that …*

Outline/Notes

1. Introduction
   introduce the topic

2. Main body
   1st paragraph: arguments contra
   - argument 1
   - argument 2, etc.
   2nd/3rd paragraph: arguments pro
   - argument 1
   - argument 2, etc.
   end with strongest argument!

4. Conclusion
   sum up your arguments
   give your opinion

TIPP: Deine Argumente wirken überzeugender, wenn du:
- dich wo möglich auf deine eigenen Erfahrungen berufst, in dem du z. B. eigene Erlebnisse einbringst: *In my experience …,*
- Fakten (Quellen, Experten, Statistiken usw.) präsentierst: *It can't be denied that …, It's a fact that …, It goes without saying that …*

SF 8 Writing an article ➔ *SB (p. 110)*

Publikum

Für wen schreibst du? Wer ist die **Zielgruppe** deines Artikels? Wenn du z. B. einen Artikel über politische Demonstration in deiner Stadt schreibst, hast du möglicherweise andere Leser als bei einem Artikel über das letzte Spiel des lokalen Fußballvereins. Das Wissen über die Zielgruppe hilft dir, sie richtig anzusprechen und z. B. eine Überschrift zu wählen, die das Interesse dieser Leser weckt.

Aufmerksamkeit

Wie erregst du die Aufmerksamkeit möglicher Leser? Dein Artikel kann noch so gut sein – wenn ihn keiner liest, nützt das nichts. Eine gute **Überschrift** hilft, ebenso wie ein interessanter **Einstieg**. Beides kann z. B. provokant sein oder witzig – wichtig ist, dass es Leser dazu bringt, bei deinem Artikel "hängen zu bleiben". Ein gutes Mittel sind z. B. rhetorische Fragen oder ein Zitat zum Thema (ähnlich wie bei Präsentationen (➔ *SF 21*)).

Interesse

Ein Artikel funktioniert nur, wenn deine Leser auch **bis zum Ende interessiert** bleiben und nicht nach ein oder zwei Absätzen aussteigen. Halte das Interesse hoch, indem du deinen Text z. B. mit Beispielen, Anekdoten und Zitaten anreicherst. (➔ *SF 9*)

Lesbarkeit

Erleichtere das Lesen des Artikels, indem du ihn mit Zwischenüberschriften in Abschnitte unterteilst und gut strukturierst. (➔ *SF 4*) Wichtig ist eine gute Planung mithilfe einer Outline, mit der du den Artikel schon vorstrukturierst. (➔ *SF 6*) Überlege, wie du in deiner Einleitung das Interesse der Leser wecken kannst, ohne schon vorwegzunehmen, was im Rest des Artikels kommt.

TIPP: Aufmerksamkeit erregende Überschriften heißen im Internet *"clickbait"*, also Klick-Köder. Wenn du das nächste Mal Artikel suchst, achte darauf, *warum* du bestimmte Artikel liest und andere nicht: Was an den Überschriften hat dich gereizt, weiterzulesen oder den Link anzuklicken?

Abschluss

Ein guter Artikel regt die Leser auch über die Zeit des Lesens hinaus noch zum Nachdenken an. Der letzte Absatz bestimmt entscheidend den Gesamteindruck mit – der Schluss ist das, was deinen Lesern in Erinnerung bleibt und sie im besten Fall weiter beschäftigt.

Dies kannst du erreichen, in dem du z. B. nochmal auf ein Zitat in deiner Einleitung zurückkommst oder hier ein weiteres anbringst. Wenn du im ersten Absetz eine rhetorische Frage gestellt hast, kannst du im letzten Absatz diese beantworten oder noch einmal stellen. Oder du stellst eine weiterführende Frage, die sich aus dem Informationen in deinem Artikel ergibt.

TIPP: Ein Artikel ist **kein Aufsatz**, bei dem du in der Einleitung die Fragestellung wiederholst und andeutest, wie du sie lösen willst. Bei einem Artikel geht es eher darum, in der Einleitung das Interesse der Leser zu wecken und sie zum Weiterlesen oder Nachdenken zu bewegen.

SF 9 Writing an opinion piece/a comment ➔ *SB (p. 111)*

Planungsphase

Step 1: Sammle Ideen und mache erste Notizen. Was willst du sagen? Was willst du erreichen? Welche Fakten oder Zitate unterstützen deine Meinung? Hast du schon eine Lösungsidee, von der du andere überzeugen möchtest?

Step 2: Überlege dir eine gute Überschrift. Sie sollte die Aufmerksamkeit der Leser wecken und sie neugierig machen.

Step 3: Erstelle eine Outline. (➔ *SF 6*) Überlege, wie du deine Argumentation/Meinung unterstützen kannst (Fakten, Statistiken, Zitate etc.).

Step 4: Recherchiere passendes Material. (➔ *SF 30*)

Schreibphase

Step 1: Beginne dein *opinion piece* mit einem kurzen Absatz zu dem Thema und deiner Meinung dazu.

Step 2: Präsentiere Argumente für deine Meinung in den folgenden Absätzen und ergänze sie mit weiteren Fakten, Beispielen oder Zitaten. Dabei kannst du viele der Redemittel verwenden, die du auch bei einer Erörterung nutzt. (➔ *SF 7*)

- Benutze das **simple present** für generelle Aussagen und das **simple present** oder **simple past** für die Beispiele, Anekdoten etc., die deine Meinung stützen.
- Verwende Überzeugungstechniken. Das sind z. B.
  - **Personalpronomen**, um den Text persönlicher zu machen: mit **you** sprichst du Leser direkt an, mit **we** stellst du eine Gemeinsamkeit her und mit **I** unterstreichst du, dass es sich um deine Meinung handelt.
  - **Zitate, Anekdoten, Statistiken** stützen deine Meinung: Zitate zeigen, dass andere Menschen deine Meinung teilen, Anekdoten bringen deine Punkte den Lesern näher und Statistiken belegen, dass deine Meinung auf Fakten beruht.
  - **Ausdrucksstarke Sprache**: schreibe abwechlungsreich (➔ *SF 5*) und verwende Wörter, die emotional ansprechen, wie z. B. Adjektive und Adverbien, die den Leser wütend oder glücklich, traurig oder fröhlich machen
  - **Rhetorische Fragen**: mit Fragen, auf die eigentlich keine Antwort erwartet wird, kannst du deine Aussage nochmal unterstreichen: *Is climate change real? Is killing wrong? Who can deny this?*

Step 3: Im letzten Absatz, der *conclusion*, wiederholst du noch einmal deine Meinung und schlägst entweder eine Lösung vor (wenn es sich z. B. um ein Problem handelt) oder forderst deine Leser auf, etwas zu tun.

Outline/Notes

1. Headline
catch your readers' attention (clear statement, provocative question etc.)

2. First paragraph
- state your topic AND your opinion clearly (keep it short!)
- keep your readers interested

3. Supporting paragraphs
use statistics, facts, quotes etc. to back up your main statement

4. Final paragraph/Conclusion
- restate your opinion
- suggest a solution or call for action

TIPP: Übertreibe es nicht mit den Statistiken, Anekdoten und Zitaten, sondern konzentriere dich auf besonders interessante oder spannende Punkte wie z. B. Zahlen, die dich in einer Statistik selber überrascht haben.

SF 10 Writing a report ➔ SB (p. 112)

Struktur
Wie jeder Text sollte ein Bericht aus einer **Überschrift**, einer **Einleitung**, einem **Hauptteil** und einem **Schluss** bestehen. (➔ *SF 4*)

In einer Gliederung (➔ *SF 6*) kannst du diese Struktur schon anlegen und für jeden Textteil eine Überschrift notieren sowie Stichwörter dazu ergänzen. Wenn du viele Informationen im Hauptteil unterbringen möchtest, verwende auch Unterüberschriften.

Stichwörter
In der **Einleitung** eines Berichtes sagst du kurz, was passiert ist. Dabei kannst du schon knapp die wichtigsten ***wh*-Fragen** beantworten, bevor du im Hauptteil näher darauf eingehst.

In deiner Gliederung (➔ *SF 6*) solltest du deswegen für die Einleitung deine Stichworte auf die Fragen **Who?**, **What?**, **When?**, **Where?** und **Why?** konzentrieren.

Im **Hauptteil** eines Berichtes stehen dann die **Details** des Ereignisses, meist in chronologischer Reihenfolge. Hier werden also die *wh*-Fragen genauer beantwortet, deswegen solltest du in der Gliederung für den Hauptteil weitere Stichworte zu den einzelnen Fragen sammeln.

Im **Schlussabsatz** bringst du deinen Bericht zum Abschluss, indem du z. B. kurz das Ergebnis oder die Folgen des beschriebenen Ereignisses darstellst.

TIPP: Ein Bericht soll objektiv sein und Fakten darstellen. Konzentriere dich bei deinen *keywords* in der Gliederung darauf, die 5 *wh*-Fragen zu beantworten:
- **What** happened?
- **Who** did what?
- **When** did it happen?
- **Where** did it happen?
- **Why** did it happen?

Denk daran, dass ein Bericht im *simple past* geschrieben wird. Du solltest also deine Stichworte auch gleich so notieren.

SF 11 Writing a summary ➔ SB (pp. 112–113)

Planungsphase
Step 1: Lies den Text genau. Mach dir Notizen (➔ *SF 39*) oder markiere wichtige Stellen im Text (➔ *SF 2*).

Step 2: Beantworte die *wh*-Fragen **Who? What? Where? When? Why?** zum Text. Du kannst dir dazu Stichworte am Rand machen.

Who? Who does something? Who is the text about?
What? What happens? What does person X do?
Where? Where does it take place?
When? When does it take place?
Why? Why does person X act this way?
Why does something happen?

Step 3: Entscheide, welche Textteile wichtige Informationen enthalten. Beispiele, Vergleiche, direkte Rede oder Zahlen und Ähnliches gehören nicht in eine Zusammenfassung.

TIPP: Du kannst Teile, die für deine Zusammenfassung überflüssig sind, im Text einklammern.

Schreibphase
Step 1: Schreib einen ersten Entwurf.
- Beginne mit der Einleitung, in der wichtige Informationen wie Titel, Autor/in, Thema und Hauptaussage des Textes stehen. Wenn du einen Artikel zusammenfasst, solltest du hier die Quelle nennen.
- Verwende immer das **simple present**.
- Kopiere nicht den Text, sondern benutze deine eigenen Worte.
- Wichtig: gib nie deine eigene Meinung oder Wertung.

Step 2: Überarbeite deine Zusammenfassung.
- Hast du alle wichtigen Aspekte genannt und unwichtige Details weggelassen?
- Ist der Text durchgängig *im simple present?*
- Vergiss nicht, Rechtschreibung/Grammatik zu prüfen. (➔ *SF 14*)

LANGUAGE HELP: Folgende *phrases* können dir bei der Einleitung helfen:
- The story/text is about …
- The text deals with …
- The topic of the text is …
- The article/text shows …

SF 12 Writing a review ➜ *SB (p. 113)*

Vorbereitung

Step 1: Lies das Buch bzw. gucke den Film. Notiere dir, was dir besonders auffällt – positiv, negativ oder einfach als bemerkenswert.

Step 2: Ergänze deine Notizen mit Informationen über das Buch bzw. den Film. Am besten strukturierst du die Notizen gleich, z. B. in einer Tabelle. Folge dabei schon der Struktur der Rezension (siehe rechts).

Schreibphase

Step 1: Schreibe einen ersten Entwurf.

- Verwende das **simple present**.
- Beginne mit der **Einleitung**, die die grundlegenden Informationen enthält.
- Im **Hauptteil** schreibe mithilfe deiner Notizen eine kurze Zusammenfassung des Inhalts (ohne zuviel zu verraten – besonders nicht das Ende) und gib mehr Informationen zu den Charakteren.
- Am **Schluss** gib deine Meinung zum Buch oder Film. Sage, weshalb du glaubst, dass man das Buch lesen/den Film sehen sollte (oder nicht). Eventuell erwähne, für welche Zielgruppe das Buch/der Film gedacht ist.
- Falls du es noch nicht getan hast, überlege dir eine **Überschrift**, die das Interesse der Leser weckt.

Step 2: Überarbeite deinen Text. (➜ *SF 14, SF 15*)

Headline	• *catch your readers' attention* • *hint at your opinion or the book's/movie's content*
Introduction	• *title, author/director, year, length (pages/minutes), setting* • *basic information: genre/type of movie/book (action, drama, comedy), characters, one-sentence summary of plot*
Main part	• *short summary of the plot (but don't reveal too much!)* • *more information about characters (and cast if you're writing about a movie)*
Conclusion	• *your opinion, e. g. on characters, plot, actors, dialogue, special effects, the message of the book/movie, …* • *recommendation; who is the target group? (e. g. young adults, comedy fans, people who like drama/romance)*

TIPP: Verwende in deiner Beschreibung starke Adjektive und Adverbien, um deine Leser entweder von dem Buch/Film zu überzeugen oder abzuschrecken (an **action-packed** thriller, a **hilarious** comedy, a **highly** entertaining movie, a **boring** drama with **one-dimensional** characters …).

SF 13 Writing a formal letter or email ➜ *SB (p. 114)*

Schreibe **deine Adresse** (ohne Namen) oben rechts.
Verwende keine typisch deutschen Buchstaben wie ä, ö, ü oder ß.

Schreibe die volle Anschrift (mit Namen, wenn du ihn weißt) des **Adressaten** auf die linke Seite.

Schreibe das **Datum** auf die rechte Seite.

Sage kurz im **Betreff**, worum es im Brief geht.

Beginne deinen Brief mit *Dear Sir or Madam*, wenn du keinen genauen Ansprechpartner hast.
Ansonsten schreibe *Dear Mr/Mrs/Ms …* (ohne Komma danach!).
Fange danach immer groß an.

Nenne den **Grund des Schreibens** im ersten Absatz.

- Ergänze weitere Informationen in den folgenden Absätzen.
- Verwende **Langformen** (*I am/We are/I would*) statt **Kurzformen** (*I'm/We're/I'd*) und Abkürzungen.

Wenn du den Adressaten um etwas bittest (z. B. Informationen), **bedanke dich** im Voraus.

Beende den Brief mit *Yours faithfully* wenn du den Namen des Ansprechpartners kennst; ansonsten schreibe *Yours sincerely*.
Tippe deinen Namen am Ende des Briefes, aber lasse ausreichend Platz für deine **Unterschrift**.

Kruemelstrasse 12
12345 Berlin
Germany

John Keats
Donne House
Ipswich IP3 4BA
United Kingdom

3 March 2016

Enquiry about exchange programme

Dear Mr Keats

I am writing to enquire about the exchange programme which I saw advertised in The English Magazine.

I have been studying English at school for five years now and I would like to take part in an exchange programme to improve my English.

Could you please tell me if you offer any exchange programmes for one month in the summer? It would be helpful to know about dates, application procedures and the cost of such an exchange. Any additional information would be very welcome.

Thank you for your help. I look forward to hearing from you soon.

Yours sincerely,

Paul Panther

Paul Panther

TIPP: Bei einer formellen E-Mail brauchst du Datum und Adressaten nicht zu nennen. Ansonsten gelten dieselben Regeln wie bei einem formellen Brief. Liste am Ende der Mail deine Kontaktdaten auf (Name, Adresse, ggf. Telefonnummer). Ganz wichtig: verwende auf keinen Fall Emoticons oder Smileys.

SF 14 Revising texts ➜ *SB (p. 115)*

Textüberarbeitung

1. Stimmt die Struktur? (➜ *SF 4*)
   Jeder Text braucht
   - eine Einleitung, die in das Thema einführt,
   - einen Hauptteil, der das Thema ausführt,
   - einen Schluss, der alles auf den Punkt bringt.
2. Stimmt der Aufbau der Absätze? (➜ *SF 4*)
   Jeder Absatz
   - befasst sich mit einem zusammenhängenden Gedanken,
   - beginnt mit einem *topic sentence*, der diesen Gedanken einführt.
3. Stimmen die Verknüpfungen? (➜ *SF 5*)
   Gute *linking words*
   - schaffen Verbindungen zwischen Sätzen oder Satzteilen,
   - helfen, Zusammenhänge besser darzustellen und verständlich zu machen.
4. Sind die Zeitangaben richtig gesetzt? (➜ *SF 5*)
   Time markers
   - helfen, sich z. B. in einer Geschichte zurechtzufinden,
   - machen das Geschehen anschaulicher.
5. Enthält der Text Adjektive und Adverbien? (➜ *SF 5*)
   Adjektive und Adverbien
   - erlauben nähere Beschreibungen von Personen und Dingen,
   - machen Texte anschaulicher.
6. Hat der Text sprachliche/grammatikalische Fehler?
   Überprüfe deinen Text
   - auf Rechtschreibung,
   - auf grammatische Formen, z. B. Verbformen, Satzbau (*word order*) usw.

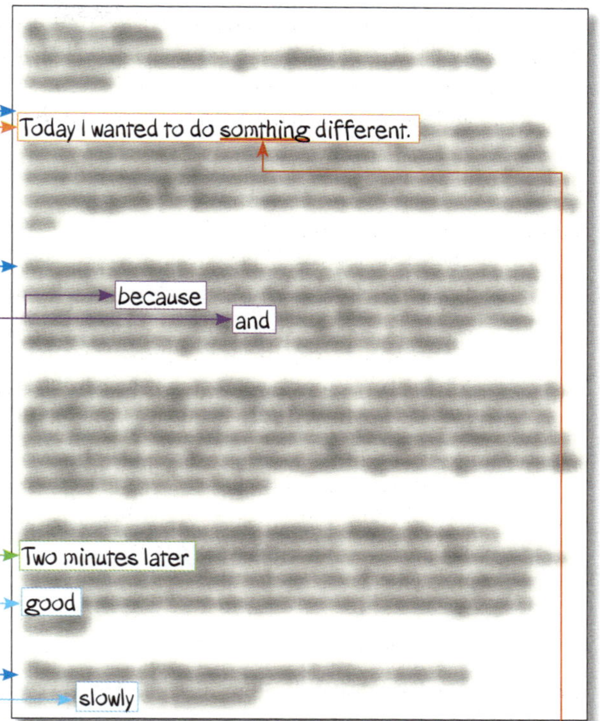

Fehlerprotokoll

Die Fehler in einem Text zu korrigieren ist eine Sache, aber besser wäre es natürlich, dieselben Fehler nicht zu wiederholen.

Dabei hilft ein Fehlerprotokoll. Darin notierst du Fehler, die du immer wieder machst. Dieses Fehlerprotokoll kann ein Heft sein, ein Karteikasten oder auch eine Sammlung von Notizzetteln, die du dir über deinen Schreibtisch hängst.

Hauptsache, es ist etwas, das du immer schnell zur Hand hast, wenn du zu Hause einen Text schreiben oder überarbeiten sollst.

TIPP: Häufige Fehlerquellen sind z. B.
- Groß-/Kleinschreibung
- Wörter, die gleich klingen, aber unterschiedlich geschrieben werden: *your/you're, their/they're/there*
- Verwendung des Apostrophs
- Bildung der Zeitformen der Verben: *stop ➜ stopping, try ➜ tries*
- Wörter mit „stummen" Buchstaben: *walk, talk, know*

SF 15 Revising and improving electronic texts ➜ *SB (p. 116)*

Korrektur

- Nutze die Überprüfungsfunktion deines Textverarbeitungsprogramms.
  Aber: sieh dir alle gemeldeten Fehler genau an, denn nicht alles, was als falsch angezeigt wird, ist auch wirklich falsch.
- Lies deinen Text trotz der Überprüfung durch das Programm noch einmal Korrektur, denn nicht alle Fehler werden auch als solche erkannt (z. B. wenn ein Tippfehler zu einem anderen korrekten Wort führt, das aber im Kontext nicht passt wie **the win in the trees** statt **the wind in the trees**).

Layout

- Lass genügend Abstand an den **Rändern** (normalerweise reichen die voreingestellten Ränder in deinem Textverarbeitungsprogramm, also 2,5 cm).
- Richte den Text **linksbündig** aus, denn das ist am besten lesbar (Ausnahme: die Überschrift kann zentriert sein, ebenso wie z. B. ein Zitat zum Einstieg).
- **Zwischenüberschriften** lockern den Text auf und machen das Lesen leichter, weil sie größere Textblöcke unterteilen.
- Überlege dir gut, wo du **Bilder** einbaust und welche Größe sie haben sollen: Bilder, die einen Inhalt im Text veranschaulichen, sollten auch möglichst nah an dieser Textstelle platziert werden. Die Größe solltest du so wählen, dass die der Inhalt gut zu erkennen ist. Gib immer die **Quelle** an, wenn du ein Bild verwendest, v. a. wenn möglich auch den Namen des Urhebers/der Urheberin. (➜ *SF33*, *SF34*)

Formatierung

- Wähle eine gut lesbare **Schriftart**. Benutze diese Schrift für den kompletten Text. Für Überschriften oder Bildunterschriften kannst du auch eine andere Schrift verwenden (aber es sollten auf keinen Fall mehr als drei verscheidene Schriftarten sein).
- Die **Schriftgröße** sollte so groß sein, dass der Text gut lesbar ist (z. B. 12 pt). Das gilt auch für den **Zeilenabstand**.
- Zur Hervorhebung bestimmter Textstellen, z. B. Zitaten, Songtiteln, Buchtiteln, Namen etc., kannst du verschiedene **Schriftstile** wie **fett**, *kursiv* oder <u>unterstrichen</u> verwenden. Du solltest aber sparsam damit umgehen, damit der Text nicht unübersichtlich wird und auch nicht alles gleichzeitig verwenden.

TIPP: Wenn dein Text der Öffentlichkeit zugänglich gemacht wird, z. B. auf der Schulwebseite, musst du vor der Verwendung von Bildern die Urheber um Erlaubnis fragen. (➜ *SF34*)

TIPP: Bei **Schriften** unterscheidet man zwischen **serifen** (z. B. Times New Roman) und **serifenlosen** (z. B. Arial). Für **längere Texte**, besonders wenn sie gedruckt sind, nimmt man in der Regel serife Schriften. **Kürzere Texte** und solche, die vor allem am Bildschirm gelesen werden, wirken durch serifenlose Schriften oft lesbarer.

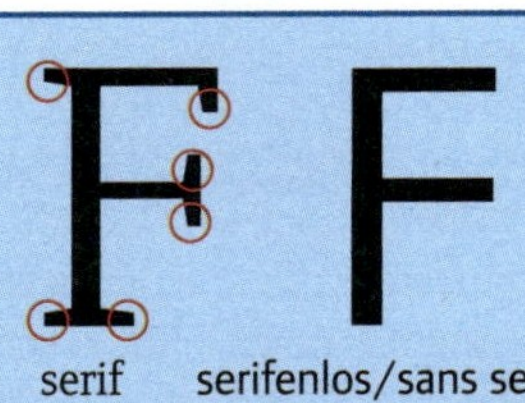

SF 16 Communicating in everyday situations ➜ SB (p. 117)

Step 1: Beginne freundlich, z. B. mit etwas, was beide Gesprächspartner verbindet (der Ort, die Situation usw.).

Step 2: Halte die Unterhaltung am Laufen:
- zeige dein Interesse, indem du Fragen stellst
- vermeide einsilbige Antworten, um nicht desinteressiert oder unfreundlich zu wirken
- wenn du etwas nicht verstehst, frage nach
- wenn du etwas nicht sagen kannst, versuche es zu umschreiben oder bitte deinen Gesprächspartner um Hilfe

Step 3: Beende das Gespräch so freundlich, wie du es angefangen hast:
- bedanke dich, wenn du um Hilfe gebeten hast
- verabschiede dich freundlich

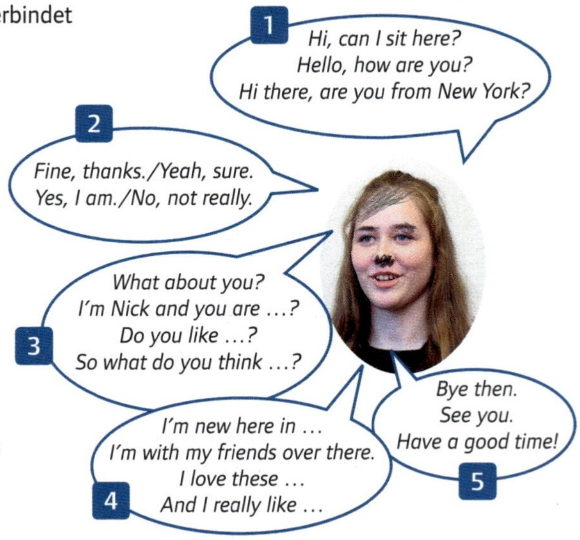

TIPP: Mach dir vor dem Gespräch klar, mit wem du redest. Mit anderen Jugendlichen kannst du häufig viel informeller sprechen als mit älteren Menschen. Überlege auch, ob es kulturelle Unterschiede gibt (➜ *SF25*) und ob es Dinge gibt, die du deswegen beachten musst.

SF 17 Having a discussion ➜ SB (p. 118)

Vorbereitungsphase

Step 1: Bereite dich auf das Thema vor: Recherchiere Fakten und Beispiele und überlege, was deine Meinung zu dem Thema ist. Mache dir Notizen.

Step 2: Halte deine Notizen für die Diskussion bereit – z. B. auf kleinen Zetteln – damit du darauf zugreifen kannst, falls du sie brauchst.

Step 3: Überlege dir vorher ein Statement, das deine Meinung zum Thema gut ausdrückt; das erleichtert den Einstieg in die Diskussion.

TIPP: Bei Rollenspielen musst du manchmal eine Meinung vertreten, die anders ist als deine eigene. Dann kannst du in deinen Notizen z. B. versuchen, Argumente und Gegenargumente einander gegenüberzustellen, um dann in der Diskussion schnell und gut reagieren zu können.

Diskussion

Step 1: Starting the discussion:
Sage deine Meinung (z. B. mithilfe der Eröffnung, die du dir überlegt hast).

Step 2: Continuing the discussion:
Tausche deine Meinung mit anderen aus. Bleibe höflich und sachlich. Hör den anderen zu und lass sie ausreden.
- Wenn du sprichst, beziehe dich auf die Anderen und sage, weshalb du ihren Argumenten zustimmst (oder nicht).
- Stütze deine Meinung mit Fakten und Beispielen.

Step 3: Ending the discussion:
- Fasse deinen Standpunkt noch einmal knapp zusammen.
- Versuche, Gemeinsamkeiten festzustellen (v. a. wenn es darum geht, sich auf etwas zu einigen) oder einigt euch darüber, dass es nicht eine gemeinsame Lösung gibt **(agree to disagree)**.
- Falls gefordert, einigt euch auf eine Lösung oder einen Kompromiss.

TIPP: Im Englischen ist man häufig weit weniger direkt als im Deutschen. Das bedeutet, dass du bei Diskussionen
- besonders gut zuhören musst, weil du sonst evtl. nicht genau mitbekommst, ob man dir zustimmt oder widerspricht
- kurze, zu direkte Antworten wie *"No."* vermeiden solltest, weil die unhöflich wirken.

SF 18 Agreeing and disagreeing with people's opinions ➔ *SB (p. 118)*

LANGUAGE HELP: Es ist bei Diskussionen hilfreich, einige Standard-Redewendungen parat zu haben. Wenn du die beherrscht, kannst du dich mehr auf deine Argumente konzentrieren. Folgende Phrasen solltest du dir aufschreiben und sie lernen:

Stating your opinion
- *In my opinion …*
- *Well, I'd say …*
- *It's a fact that …*
- *Personally, I think…*
- *If you ask me …*
- *I think/feel/believe …*
- *First of all, I'd like to point out…*
- *I'm certain that …*

Agreeing
- *I agree …*
- *Exactly./Absolutely./…*
- *You're quite right.*
- *I think so too.*
- *You've got a good point there.*
- *That's exactly how I see it.*
- *That's true/right.*
- *I couldn't agree with you more.*

Disagreeing
- *I'm afraid I don't quite agree …*
- *I'm not sure about that.*
- *Do you really think so?*
- *I'm not convinced that …*
- *I doubt that (very much).*
- *I don't agree with you at all.*
- *I disagree (completely).*
- *It's not as simple as that.*

SF 19 Preparing and taking part in a panel discussion ➔ *SB (p. 119)*

Vorbereitungsphase

Step 1: Bereite dich auf die Diskussion vor wie auf andere Diskussionen auch: Recherchiere Fakten und überlege, was deine Meinung zu dem Thema ist. Mache dir Notizen.

Step 2: Halte deine Notizen für die Diskussion bereit – z. B. auf kleinen Zetteln – damit du darauf zugreifen kannst, falls du sie brauchst.

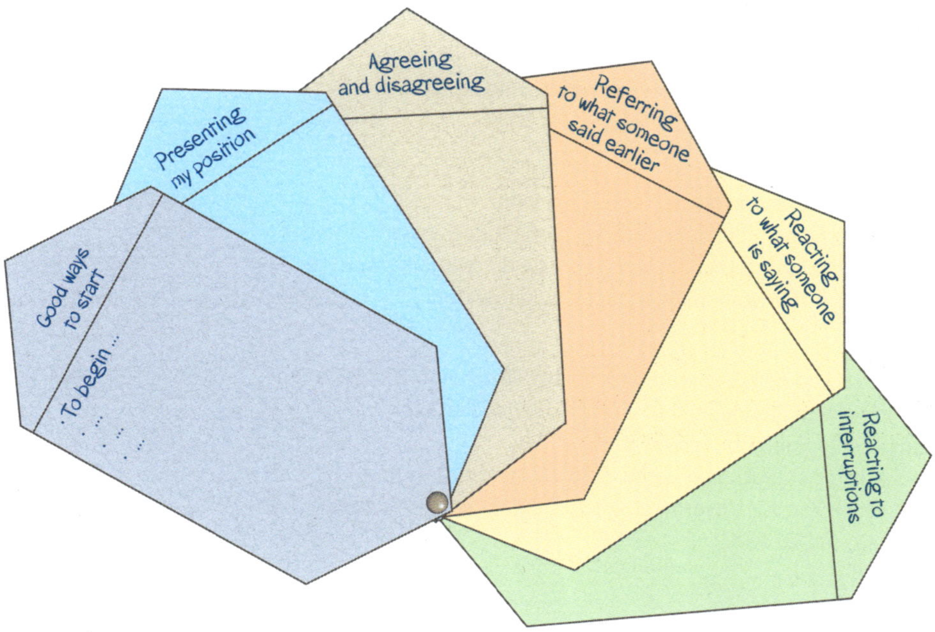

Step 3: Bereite dich auf deine Rolle in der Diskussion vor – Moderator, Diskussionsteilnehmer oder Zuhörer. Jede Rolle hat andere Aufgaben.
Nützliche Redemittel (➜ *SF 18*) können auf einem **discussion fan** notiert werden, damit sie schnell zur Hand sind.

Moderator/in

Die Moderatorin/Der Moderator einer Podiumsdiskussion
- überlegt sich im Vorfeld der Diskussion mögliche Fragen für die Teilnehmer
- stellt kurz die Diskussionsteilnehmer vor
- leitet die Diskussion und stellt Fragen, wenn die Diskussion stockt
- sorgt dafür, dass sich alle Beteiligten an die Regeln halten und dass alle Teilnehmer etwa gleich viel Redezeit haben
- achtet auf die Zeit oder bestimmt einen *timekeeper*, der dies tut
- ermuntert die Zuhörer, Fragen zu stellen und moderiert diese.

Diskussionsteilnehmer/in

Die Teilnehmer einer Podiumsdiskussion
- sind gut vorbereitet: sie haben sich ihre eigenen Argumente notiert und sich Gedanken zu den möglichen Argumenten der anderen Teilnehmer gemacht
- geben zu Beginn der Diskussion ein kurzes Statement, das ihre Meinung knapp zusammenfasst
- folgen der Diskussion aufmerksam und notieren sich Argumente der anderen Teilnehmer, um darauf reagieren zu können.

Zuhörer/in

Die Zuhörer bei einer Podiumsdiskussion
- überlegen sich im Vorfeld, welche Argumente sie zu bestimmten Themen erwarten und überlegen sich entsprechende Fragen/Kommentare
- können sich im Anschluss an die Diskussion dazu äußern, welche Argumente sie am überzeugendsten fanden
- machen sich während der Diskussion Notizen, um im Anschluss Fragen zu stellen oder die Argumente kommentieren zu können.

Durchführung

Eine Podiumsdiskussion sollte einen vorher vereinbarten Zeitrahmen nicht überschreiten (z. B. 30 Minuten). Im Anschluss daran sollte Zeit für Fragen und Kommentare der Zuhörer eingeplant werden. Für die Einhaltung der Zeit und der Diskussionsregeln ist der Moderator/die Moderatorin verantwortlich.

SF 20 Taking part in an interview ➜ *SB (p. 120)*

Prepare

- Finde so viel wie möglich über den Job und den Arbeitgeber heraus.
- Notiere mögliche Fragen, die du dem Arbeitgeber stellen kannst.
- Überlege dir aber auch, welche Fragen man dir stellen könnte und bereite Antworten darauf vor.

Practise

- Übe das Bewerbungsgespräch mit einem Partner/einer Partnerin.
- Gib deinem Übungspartner die Fragen, die du von deinem Arbeitgeber erwartest und beantworte sie. Sage deinem Übungspartner auch, dass er/sie dir ruhig unerwartete Fragen stellen soll. So übst du, auf unvorbereitete Fragen zu antworten.

Present

- Überlege dir im Vorfeld, was du zu dem Bewerbungsgespräch anziehen möchtest. Besprich das ruhig auch mit einem Freund/einer Freundin oder deinen Eltern. Die Auswahl der Kleidung hängt vom Arbeitgeber ab.
- Stelle sicher, dass du pünktlich bist. Suche dir vorher heraus, wie du zum Ort des Gespräches kommst. Plane Zeit für Unvorhergesehenes ein. Es ist immer besser, zehn Minuten zu früh als zu spät zu sein.

Participate

- Stelle dich am Anfang vor, am besten mit einem freundlichen Lächeln.
- Lass dir Zeit, Fragen zu beantworten, besonders wenn es unerwartete Fragen sind. Antworte nicht mit "Yes." oder "No.", sondern versuche, Fragen ausführlich und höflich zu beantworten.
- Wenn du eine Frage nicht verstehst, frag nach.
- Am Ende des Gespräches, verabschiede dich mit einem freundlichen Lächeln und bedanke dich für das Gespräch.

TIPP: Achte auch auf deine non-verbale Kommunikation – wie du stehst, gehst, sitzt – und siehe deinem Gegenüber in die Augen.

LANGUAGE HELP: Folgender Wortschatz hilft dir …

- **bei der Begrüßung**
  Nice to meet you too. / Thank you for inviting me today. / I'm fine, thank you.
- **über dich selbst zu sprechen:**
  Well, I'm 16 years old and … / Actually, one of my main strengths is …
- **zu erklären, was du meinst:**
  What I mean is … / What I'm really trying to say is … I'm glad you asked that question because … / … is very important to me, as is …
- **weitere Punkte anzubringen:**
  Another point I should mention is … / There's something else I'd like to say. / Let me explain that in some more detail.
- **aufmerksam zu wirken:**
  I see./Right./Uhuh.
- **bei Unklarheiten nachzufragen:**
  Sorry, I don't quite understand. / Sorry, but do you mean … / I am not sure I have understood your question correctly. / Sorry, could you rephrase that?
- **bei der Verabschiedung:**
  Thank you for the chance to speak to you.

SF 21 Giving a presentation ➜ *SB (p. 121)*

Vorbereitung der Präsentation

Step 1: **Recherchiere** dein Thema (➜ *SF 30*) und mach dir Notizen, am besten gleich auf Englisch. (➜ *SF 39*)

Step 2: **Strukturiere** die Informationen, z. B. mit einer Gliederung. (➜ *SF 6*)

Step 3: Wähle eine **Form der Präsentation** aus, die das Thema gut veranschaulicht (Poster, Folie, …). Gestalte dein Poster/deine Folie und beachte dabei die Grundsätze für ein gutes Poster.

Step 4: Bereite deine **Notizen** für die Präsentation vor, z. B. auf nummerierten Karteikarten. Verwende keine ganzen Sätze, sondern Stichworte, Symbole oder Halbsätze. Notiere dir z. B. auch schwierige Wörter und ihre Aussprache.

Step 5: Überlege dir einen guten Einstieg wie z. B eine rhetorische Frage oder ein Zitat, um die Aufmerksamkeit der Zuhörer zu wecken

Step 6: Wenn ihr in einem Team arbeitet, entscheidet gemeinsam, wer welchen Teil der Präsentation übernimmt. (➜ *SF 28*)

Step 7: **Übe deine Präsentation** zu Hause vor einem Spiegel oder vor einem kleinen Publikum (Eltern, Großeltern, Freunde).

TIPP: Um ein **gutes Poster** zu gestalten, solltest du folgendes beachten:
- Wähle eine passende Überschrift.
- Schreibe groß und für alle gut lesbar.
- Ergänze passende Bilder, um den Text/die Inhalte zu veranschaulichen.

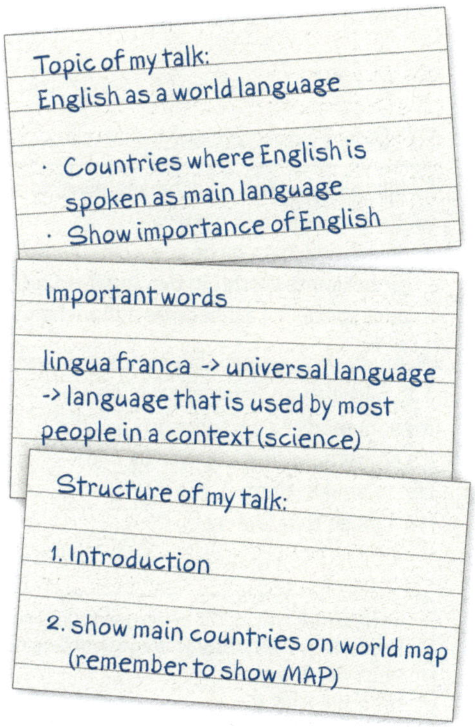

Halten der Präsentation

Step 1: **Warte, bis es ruhig ist.** Schau die Zuhörer/innen an. Erkläre, worüber du sprechen wirst und wie deine Präsentation aufgebaut ist.

Step 2: **Sprich langsam** und deutlich und möglichst frei. Lies nicht von deinen Notizen ab.

Step 3: Beende deine Präsentation mit einer kleinen **Zusammenfassung** der wichtigsten Punkte. Bedanke dich fürs Zuhören und beantworte Fragen zu deinem Vortrag.

SF 22 Mediating written or spoken information ➔ *SB (p. 122)*

Mediation von schriftlichen oder mündlichen Informationen

Wenn du Informationen in einer anderen Sprache wiedergeben sollst, geht es nicht darum, alles zu übersetzen, sondern es kommt darauf an, die wichtigsten Informationen herauszusuchen. Oft stellt dir die Person, für die du die Informationen wiedergibst, gezielte Fragen – so weißt du, worauf du achten musst.

Schriftliche Informationen

- **Scanne** den Text gezielt nach den geforderten Informationen. (➔ *SF 1*)
- Mach dir keine Sorgen, wenn du nicht jedes Wort verstehst. Das ist oft nicht nötig, um die wichtigen Punkte zu verstehen und wiederzugeben.
- Wenn der Text länger ist und du viele Informationen im Blick behalten musst, **markiere** die wichtigsten Textstellen. (➔ *SF 2*)
- Mach dir **Notizen** in deinen eigenen Worten. (➔ *SF 39*)

Mündliche Informationen

- Achte beim Hören gezielt auf die gesuchten Informationen. (➔ *SF 27*)
- Mach dir Notizen. (➔ *SF 39*)
- Überlege, wie du deine Notizen am besten in der anderen Sprache wiedergeben kannst

TIPP: Bei **Mediation im Unterricht** hast du in der Regel eine Aufgabenstellung, die dir sagt, worauf du beim Lesen oder Hören achten musst bzw. welche Stellen du wiedergeben sollst. Konzentriere dich beim Lesen des Textes auf diese Stellen (*scanning*) bzw. mache dir gezielt zu diesen Stellen Notizen.

TIPP: Wenn du den Inhalt eines Texts schriftlich in einer anderen Sprache wiedergeben sollst, achte darauf, dass deine Mediation nicht länger ist als ca. 35–40 % des Originaltextes, ähnlich wie bei einer *summary*. (➔ *SF 11*)

SF 23 Selecting relevant information *SB (p. 122)*

- **Analysiere die Situation**, um abzuschätzen, um welche Informationen es gehen könnte (Restaurant, Bahnhof, Flughafen usw.).
- Wenn du unsicher bist, **frage nach**.
- **Übersetze** wichtige Stichworte direkt, wenn du die Wörter kennst.
- **Umschreibe Begriffe**, die du nicht kennst. (➔ *SF 24*)

TIPP: Wenn du Informationen wiedergibst, kannst du oft Details zu einem Begriff zusammenfassen. Wenn z. B. in einem Text *Twitter*, *Facebook* und *Pinterest* vorkommen, kannst du *social media* sagen anstatt alle aufzuzählen.

SF 24 Paraphrasing ➔ *SB (p. 123)*

Es fällt dir eventuell manchmal schwer, Informationen in Englisch wiederzugeben, z. B. weil

- dein Wortschatz nicht ausreicht,
- dir bekannte Wörter in der Situation nicht einfallen
- oder spezielle Fachbegriffe auftauchen.

Wenn dir das passiert, dann solltest du versuchen, diese Wörter zu umschreiben, z. B. mithilfe von Relativsätzen wie:

It's somebody/a person who …
It's something that you use to …
It's an animal that …
It's a place that/where …

LANGUAGE HELP: Oft helfen beim Umschreiben auch **Synonyme** (gleiche Bedeutung) oder **Antonyme** (gegenteilige Bedeutung). Wenn du die weißt, kannst du z. B. sagen:

- It's the same as …
- It's the opposite of …

SF 25 Dealing with cultural differences ➔ *SB (p. 123)*

Dinge, die häufig zu **Missverständnissen** führen, sind z. B.

- **Temperaturen:** 30 Grad bei uns sind heiß, in den USA eher kalt, weil in den USA Temperaturen in Fahrenheit angegeben werden, nicht in Celsius.
- **Längenangaben/Geschwindigkeit:** Bei uns wird das metrische System verwendet (Meter, Kilometer usw.), in den USA das *imperial system* mit *inch*, *yard* und *mile*. Das kann auch bei Geschwindigkeitsangaben zu Verwirrung führen, denn 75 *mph* (Meilen pro Stunde) sind z. B. ca. 120 km/h.

Am besten ist es, wenn du immer noch mal höflich nachfragst, ob dein Gegenüber alles verstanden hat. Wenn du dann feststellst, dass es zu einem Missverständnis gekommen ist, dann kannst du folgende Dinge probieren:

- Frage höflich nach, wo das Missverständnis ist. (➔ *SF 16*)
- Versuche, das Missverständnis durch eine neue Erklärung zu beseitigen.
- Ergänze deine Erläuterung evtl. mit **Hintergrundinformationen:** Es kann sein, dass du bestimmte Dinge, die für dich völlig normal sind, erklären musst (wie z. B. Mülltrennung oder das Benutzen des Nahverkehrs).
- Sei auch offen für die Erklärungen, die du evtl. im Gegenzug bekommst – hier kannst du Dinge über das Land deines Gegenübers lernen.

TIPP: Es hilft, wenn du versuchst, mögliche "Stolperstellen" schon im Vorfeld vorauszusehen.
Frage dich, was dein Gegenüber evtl. nicht oder anders verstehen könnte und erkläre diese Stellen besonders genau und evtl. auf unterschiedliche Arten.

SF 26 Viewing ➔ *SB (p. 124)*

- **Genre:**
  Handelt es sich um einen Dokumentarfilm **(documentary)**, einen Spielfilm wie z. B. **thriller**, **science-fiction/sci-fi movie**, **comedy** oder ein **drama**?
  Ist es ein Nachrichtenclip, Musikvideo oder Werbung **(commercial)**?
- **Story:**
  Wo und wann spielt der Film **(setting)**? Besetzung der Rollen **(cast)**, Schauplatz **(location)**, Handlung **(plot)**.
- **Camera:**
  Erst durch die Bilder der **Kamera** ist der Zuschauer in der Lage, einen Film wahrzunehmen. Die Kamera stellt das Blickfeld her und begrenzt es gleichzeitig, z. B. hinsichtlich der Beziehung der Charaktere zueinander. Auch die Stimmung oder Spannung in einer Szene wird von der Kameraführung beeinflusst.
  Dafür gibt es z. B. folgende Mittel:
  - **Shots:** Die **Kameraeinstellung** beeinflusst, was man sieht und wie man Szenen wahrnimmt, ob z. B. Personen in Nahaufnahme **(close-up)**, der mittleren Distanz **(medium shot)** oder der Totale **(long shot)** gefilmt sind.
  - **Editing:** Filme werden meist nicht chronologisch gedreht und auch nicht nur mit einer Kamera, d. h. am Ende der Dreharbeiten müssen viele einzelne Shots zu einem Film zusammengefügt werden. Der **Filmschnitt** bestimmt die Wirkung einer Szene. Er bestimmt den Rhythmus – Einstellungen mit wenigen Schnitten wirken ruhiger, während schnelle, harte Schnitte actiongeladen wirken. Bei Nachrichten-, Dokumentar- oder Werbeclips kann der Schnitt ganz gezielt die Aussage beeinflussen.
- **Soundtrack:**
  Musik hat großen Einfluss darauf, wie man eine Szene wahrnimmt. Eine Actionszene wird oft mit schneller, lauter Musik unterlegt, eine romantische Szene eher mit ruhiger, leiser Musik. Dies geschieht, um die Wirkung des Gesehenen zu verstärken. In der Werbung wird Musik gezielt eingesetzt, um ein Produkt damit zu verknüpfen und eine emotionale Reaktion zu erwirken.

long shot

medium shot

close-up

Filmtagebuch

Wenn du eine Szene oder einen Film sehr intensiv analysieren möchtest, hilft es, ein Filmtagebuch **(viewing log)** anzulegen, in dem du die Handlung oder einzelne wichtige Szenen sowie deine Reaktion darauf festhältst.

Das Filmtagebuch kann z. B. eine einfache, zweispaltige Tabelle sein:
Spalte 1: What you noticed – images, sounds, dialogue, lighting, costumes, mood, characterization, plot, etc.
Spalte 2: Your reaction – What did you think? How did the scene make you feel?

LANGUAGE HELP: Wenn du über Filme sprechen möchtest, können dir folgende Redewendungen helfen:

- The film is about …/shows …/ tells the story of …
- The music creates/builds/supports tension/suspense/joy …
- The actor's body language helps to create a feeling of happiness/joy/ anger/suspense …
- In this scene the music/effects/ camera angle … supports the plot/ mood of the scene/…
- The camera movement creates a feeling of …
- The camera work/soundtrack helps to …
- The close-ups show his/ her feelings.

SF 27 Listening strategies ➔ *SB (pp. 125–126)*

Listening for detail

- Überleg dir vorher, auf welche Informationen du achten musst.
  - Bei einem Wetterbericht sind das z. B. Beschreibungen wie *sunny, cloudy, chance of rain* etc., bei Bahnhofsansagen z. B. Wörter wie *platform* oder Orte und Zeiten.
  - Höre dann gezielt auf solche Wörter und notiere sie. (➔ *SF 39*)
- Manchmal können auch Signalwörter helfen, dem Inhalt zu folgen und dich auf die Details zu konzentrieren:
  - Gründe, Folgen: *because, so, so that, …*
  - Vergleiche: *larger/older/… than, as … as, more, most, …*
  - Reihenfolge: *before, after, then, next, later, …*

TIPP: Im **Unterricht** kannst du Texte oft zweimal hören und hast weitere Hilfen:
- Sieh dir die Aufgabenstellung an: Was sollst du heraushören?
- Sieh dir Titel und Bilder an.
- Vergleiche nach dem Hören mit einem Partner, was ihr verstanden habt.
- Vervollständige deine Notizen sofort.

Listening for gist

- Mache dir keine Sorgen, wenn du nicht jedes Wort verstehst – das brauchst du nicht, um der Grundaussage folgen zu können. Überlege dir vorher, um was es gehen könnte (z. B. anhand des Themas) und konzentriere dich darauf.
- Versuche, von den Sachen, die du verstehst, auf Inhalte zu schließen, die noch kommen könnten.

Hörverstehenstechniken

Es gibt zwei verschiedene Techniken beim Hörverstehen:

- Bei der **bottom-up-Technik** gehst du vom Gesprochenen an das Hören heran: Konzentriere dich darauf, was gerade gesagt wird und beachte dabei z. B. die Besonderheiten verschiedener Akzente. Wie gut du das verstehst, was du in der Fremdsprache hörst, ist eine Frage der Übung.

  Du solltest beim Hören folgende Dinge beachten:
  - **Chunks/connected speech:** Im Englischen spricht man oft mehrere Wörter als Einheit aus, bei der Wortgrenzen verschwinden. Das findet man verstärkt bei
    - Ausdrücken mit Modalverben: *she'd've told me / you shouldn't've bought it / you mustabin asleep*
    - häufigen Alltagsphrasen: *Whatcha think o'that? / Howdju feel? / Dincha see it? / Whatchadoin'?*
  - Wörter, die gesprochen gleich klingen, sich in der Bedeutung aber unterscheiden:
    We'd like ice in our drinks. – We like ice in our drinks.
    I can't see them now. – I can see them now. (besonders im AE)
    Hier schafft im Gespräch gezieltes Nachfragen Sicherheit:
    Sorry, was that can or can't?

TIPP: Beim Hörverstehen hilft vor allem Übung, v. a. wenn es um **Chunks/connected speech** oder verschiedene **Dialekte und Akzente** geht. Höre dir deshalb so oft du kannst Originaltexte an, z. B. Audiobooks oder in Videos online, um ein Gefühl dafür zu entwickeln. (➔ *SF 37*)
Um dich in unterschiedliche Akzente reinzuhören und sich an sie zu "gewöhnen", kannst du z. B. Filme und Serien im Original gucken, bei denen du zur Hilfe englische Untertitel einblenden kannst.

- Bei der **top-down-Technik** gehst du von der Gesprächssituation aus an das Hören heran und versuchst, mögliche Inhalte vorherzusagen:
  - Du kannst **Gesprächsinhalte erschließen** und das Verstehen erleichtern, wenn du dir Gedanken über die Situation machst:
    - Wer redet in dieser Situation?
    - Über was wird in dieser Situation eventuell gesprochen?
    - Wie sprechen die Personen in dieser Situation miteinander?
    - Werden die Personen eher freundlich, höflich oder verärgert sein?
    - Sprechen sie in der gegeben Situation eher schnell oder langsam, eher formell oder informell?
  - Diese Vorüberlegungen helfen dir vorherzusagen, was im Gespräch gesagt wird **(prediction)**, selbst wenn du nicht jedes Wort verstehst oder durch äußere Umstände wie z. B. laute Nebengeräusche nicht hören kannst:
    It's very warm in here, isn't it? Should I open …? / It's my brother's birthday next week. I don't know what to …
  - Häufig kannst du das Thema eines Gespräches erkennen, auch wenn du nicht hörst, worum es genau geht **(inference)**. Du hörst dabei die Situation sozusagen "zwischen den Zeilen" heraus. Im folgenden Kurzdialog geht es z. B. um Essen und sehr wahrscheinlich um Pizza, ohne dass davon direkt gesprochen wird:
    Hey, do you want one slice or two? – I'll have two. Ham and extra cheese.

SF 29 Giving feedback – writing ➜ *SB (p. 127)*

- Lies den Text sorgfältig durch oder höre der Präsentation gut zu.
- Bei **Feedback zu einer Präsentation** mache dir Notizen zu den Punkten, auf die du achten sollst, z. B. Inhalt, Struktur, Sprache, Verständlichkeit des Vortrags. Wenn du einen Feedbackbogen hast, kannst du deine Notizen gleich darauf festhalten.
- Bei **Feedback zu einem Text** lies den Text genau und achte dabei besonders auf Inhalt, Struktur, Wortwahl, Grammatik und Rechtschreibung. Wenn du einen Feedbackbogen hast, mache dir darauf Notizen (siehe rechts).
- Begründe deine Einschätzungen.
- Gib dein Feedback mit **Respekt** – niemand soll sich angegriffen fühlen. Nenne erst Gelungenes und mache dann Verbesserungsvorschläge zu Punkten, die aus deiner Sicht nicht so gelungen sind.
- Wenn du Feedback bekommst, überdenke die Vorschläge gut. **Korrigiere** die Fehler, die andere gefunden haben, und arbeite an den Stellen nach, wo du eventuell Probleme hattest.

PEER FEEDBACK CHECKLIST

	☺☺	☺	😐	☹
Content				
Lena's text is:				
· interesting · exciting · funny · ________			✓	 ✓ ✓
· easy to understand.		✓		
Language				
You connected short sentences with linking words.		✓		
You connected short sentences with relative clauses.		✓		
You used different adjectives in your description of places, people and things.			✓	
You used time phrases to show the order of events.		✓		
You chose interesting words.				✓
You used adverbs.			✓	

SF 30 Finding information online ➜ *SB (p. 127)*

Step 1: Überlege dir gute **Stichwörter** für dein Thema. Je besser die Suchbegriffe sind, desto genauer sind die Ergebnisse der Suchmaschine. Die Infografik rechts hilft dir, wenn du ganz spezielle Informationen suchst.

Step 2: Nutze die **Erweiterte Suche**. Dort kannst du nicht nur festlegen, in welcher Sprache deine Ergebnisse sein sollen, sondern auch das Land eingrenzen (z. B. nur Ergebnisse aus den USA) oder die Domäne (z. B. .edu, .gov, .org).

Step 3: Sieh dir mehrere **Suchergebnisse** an, um zu sehen, ob sie passen (➜ *SF 1*).

Step 4: Achte darauf, wer die Webseite erstellt hat, um die **Qualität** der Suchergebnisse einzuschätzen.

Step 5: Speichere die besten Ergebnisse als Lesezeichen ab, damit du schnell darauf zugreifen kannst. Ordne deine Lesezeichen thematisch zur besseren Übersichtlichkeit.

Step 6: Setz dir ein **Zeitlimit** für deine Recherche und ordne dann dein Material. Prüfe, ob etwas fehlt, und suche dann ggf. gezielt nach diesen Informationen.

Step 7: Wenn du einen Text oder eine Präsentation vorbereitest, kopiere nicht einfach Inhalte von Webseiten. Mach dir **Notizen** und verwende deine eigenen Worte, um die Inhalte wiederzugeben. (➜ *SF 39*)

Internet research
Tipps und Tricks

Wenn du ganz spezifische Informationen suchst, helfen diese Tricks:

Was du suchst: Artikel aus dem *Guardian* von 2000–2014 über den Liverpool FC in der Champions League.

Wie du danach suchst:

site:theguardian.com "Liverpool FC" "champions league" 2000..2014

site:	**" "**	**..**
sucht nur auf der genannten Seite	sucht den exakten Begriff	zeigt nur Ergebnisse aus diesem Zeitraum

Was du suchst: Einen englischsprachigen Bericht, am liebsten als PDF, über den Lebensraum von Füchsen.

Wie du danach suchst:

filetype:pdf intitle:habitat of [redacted]

filetype:	**intitle:**	*****
sucht nur diesen Dateityp (pdf, doc, jpg usw.)	zeigt nur Ergebnisse, in denen dieses Wort im Titel auftaucht	sucht auch Worte wie Red Fox, Black Fox, Desert Fox usw.

SF 31 Describing and interpreting images ➜ *SB (p. 128)*

Beschreibung

Step 1: Stelle das Bild vor und sage, woher es kommt.

Step 2: Beschreibe das Bild:
- Sage, was wo zu sehen ist: *at the top/bottom / in the foreground/ background / in the middle / on the left/right*
- Geh bei der Beschreibung in einer bestimmten Reihenfolge vor, z. B. von links nach rechts oder von oben nach unten.
- Diese Präpositionen sind auch hilfreich: *behind/between/ in front of/next to/under/above*
- Beziehe dich – v. a. bei Cartoons – auch auf Bildunterschriften,- Sprechblasen, etc.: *The caption reads … / One of the characters says/thinks …*

1 *I'd like to talk about this photo of …/ cartoon …/I found it online/ in a magazine/…*

2 *In the foreground you can see … I think the people in the photo/ cartoon are talking about …*

3 *I really like/don't like the photo/cartoon because … It's interesting/boring/… because …*

4 *Thank you for listening. Do you have any questions?*

Analyse/Interpretation

Step 1: Sage, was deiner Meinung nach die Botschaft des Bildes/Cartoons ist:
- *This is a political/environmental/educational/… photo/cartoon.*
- *I think the message is …*
- *It's about …*
- *… shows that …*
- *The fact that there is … means …*
- *The picture/cartoon may be meant to show …*

Step 2: Sage, weshalb du das Bild / den Cartoon wirksam / witzig findest (oder nicht):
- *The picture/cartoon clearly shows …*
- *The message is made clear by showing/saying …*
- *I really laughed at the cartoon because it …*
- *I don't find the cartoon funny because …*
- *The picture/cartoon speaks to us directly by …*

Wenn du das Bild/den Cartoon in einer Präsentation vorstellst, musst du evtl. genauer erklären, weshalb du es/ihn ausgewählt hast oder was daran witzig ist:
- *I chose this picture because …*
- *The joke is that …*
- *It's funny because …*
- *The picture/cartoon is criticizing/making fun of …*

"Now don't forget to go on social media and rate today's lesson plan."

SF 32 Talking about statistics ➔ *SB (p. 129)*

Step 1: Identifiziere, welche Art von Diagramm du vor dir hast – **pie chart**, **bar chart**, **line graph** oder Tabelle – und sieh dir die Quelle an:
- Ist die Quelle verlässlich?
  Ist der Herausgeber z. B. ein Ministerium/eine Behörde oder eine Organisation wie *Amnesty International*?
- Sind die Angaben/Zahlen im Diagramm aktuell?
  Wenn du z. B. eine Statistik zu Kinderarmut in Großbritannien vor dir hast, ist es ein wichtiger Unterschied, ob die Zahlen von 1973 oder 2013 sind.

Step 2: Beschreibe das Diagramm/die Tabelle:
- Worum geht es? Welche Informationen gibt das Diagramm?
  The bar chart / pie chart / line graph / table … shows the different … / compares the size / number of … / is about … / contrasts … with …
- Zeigen die Daten eine Entwicklung oder werden verschiedene Zeitpunkte miteinander verglichen? *It shows … in contrast to …*
  The chart gives us information about who/what/how many/…
- Werden absolute Zahlen oder Prozentangaben verwendet?
  The chart/table shows us the number of/percentage of …
  It shows which percentage of …

Step 3: Ziehe deine Schlussfolgerungen aus dem Diagramm/der Tabelle:
My main conclusion is that … / The most important thing I've learned is that …
One thing that I hadn't realized before is …

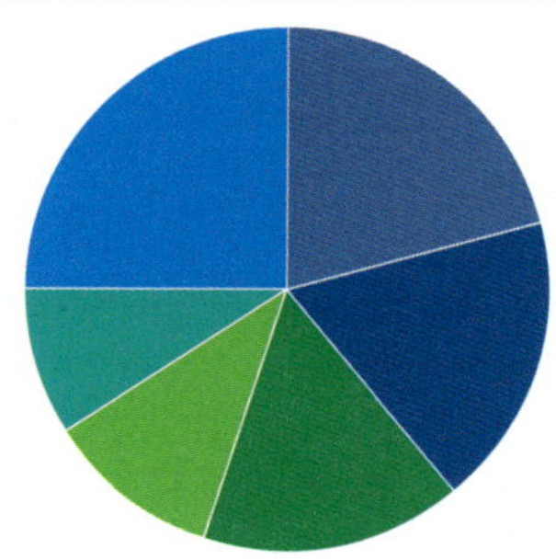

pie chart

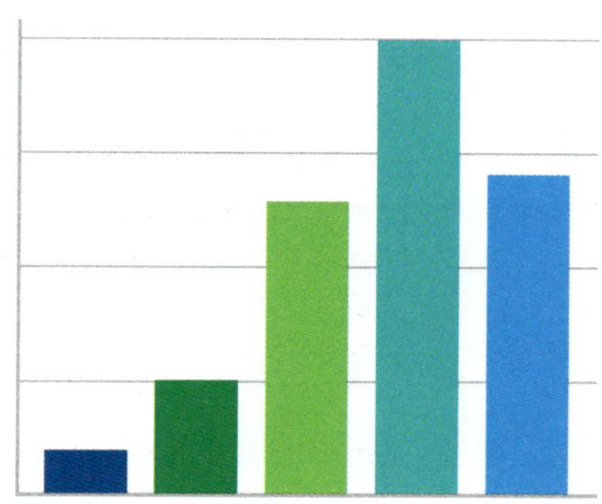

bar chart

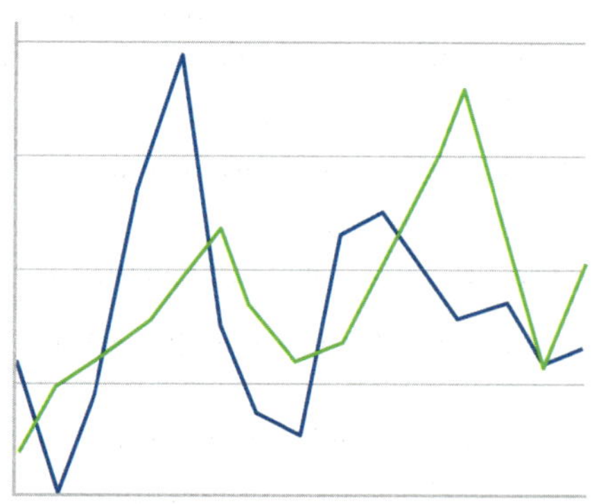

line graph

LANGUAGE HELP:
Wenn du über Diagramme sprichst, können dir folgende Redewendungen helfen:

Pie chart
- *The pie chart is divided into … segments, which show/represent …*
- *The smallest/biggest segment …*
- *The segments representing … and … constitute the majority …*
- *A huge majority/minority is …*

Bar chart
- *The bars are arranged horizontally/ vertically.*
- *There are big/vast/surprising differences between …*
- *At the top/bottom of the ranking comes …*
- *… is first/last in rank.*
- *… has the largest/second largest …*

Line graph
- *The graph shows the relationship between … and …*
- *… is twice/three times as high as …*
- *There are more than/nearly twice as many … as there are …*
- *… increase/decrease/reach a high point/rise/fall/drop/grow steadily*

SF 33 Creating a good layout for a page or poster ➜ *SB (p. 130)*

- Sortiere die **Informationen**, die du vermitteln willst: Was ist wichtig? Was ist ein Unterpunkt? Hast du Beispiele für Thesen/Argumente?
- Gib deinem Produkt eine klare **Struktur**: Texte haben meist drei Teile (Einleitung, Hauptteil, Schluss), während Poster häufig aus Aufzählungen wichtiger Punkte bestehen. Beginne für jeden neuen Gedanken einen neuen Absatz bzw. einen neuen Stichpunkt.
- Eine **Überschrift** verdeutlicht, worum es in deinem Text geht. Sie soll Leser auch neugierig machen auf das, was kommt. Wenn es in deinem Produkt um mehrere Themen/Aspekte eines Themas geht, dann kannst Du für einzelne Abschnitte auch **Zwischenüberschriften** verwenden. Das gibt dem Ganzen eine klare Struktur und hilft dem Leser, sich schnell zu orientieren.
- Ergänze dein Produkt mit **passenden Fotos, Videos, Audios, Statistiken** etc. Vergiss nicht anzugeben, woher die Medien stammen (➜ *SF 34*).
- Wenn nicht auf den ersten Blick erkennbar ist, was z. B. ein Bild zeigt, füge **Bildunterschriften** ein.
- Formatiere dein Produkt so, dass es gut lesbar ist. Dabei ist das Medium wichtig – für einen ausgedruckten Handzettel kannst du andere **Schriftarten** wählen als für einen Text, der am Bildschirm gelesen wird. (➜ *SF 15*) Für ein Poster (z. B. für einen *gallery walk*) muss die **Schriftgröße** größer sein als für einen Ausdruck. Eine große Schriftgröße hilft dir auch, nicht zu viele Punkte auf dem Poster unterzubringen – hier ist weniger mehr.

SF 35 Dealing with unknown words ➜ *SB (p. 131)*

Nachschlagen kostet Zeit und ist nicht immer nötig. Diese Tipps können dir helfen, unbekannte Wörter auch ohne ein Wörterbuch zu erschließen:

- Sieh dir die Überschrift, die Zwischenüberschriften und Bilder sowie den **Kontext** an. Beispiel: *Let's hurry. The train **departs** in ten minutes.*
- Wenn du einen **Teil des Wortes** kennst, kannst du oft die Bedeutung erschließen, z. B. *knowledge = things someone knows*
  bottle opener = something you use to open bottles
- Viele englische Wörter haben eine **Ähnlichkeit** zu deutschen Wörtern (z. B. *brochure, statue, insect*) oder Wörtern aus anderen Sprachen, z. B. *voice* (*French: voix; Latin: vox*).

TIPP: Nicht alle Wörter, die im Deutschen und Englischen ähnlich sind, haben auch dieselbe Bedeutung.
Achte daher auf **false friends**:
handy = praktisch, nicht Handy

SF 36 Using a dictionary ➜ *SB (p. 132)*

Zweisprachige Wörterbücher

Die **Leitwörter** (*running heads*) oben auf der Seite helfen dir, schnell zu finden, was du suchst. Auf der linken Seite steht das erste Stichwort, auf der rechten Seite das letzte Stichwort der Doppelseite.

- *resign* ist das **Stichwort** (*headword*). Stichwörter sind alphabetisch geordnet: *r* vor *s*, *ra* vor *re*, *rhe* vor *rhi* usw.
- Die **kursiv gedruckten** Hinweise helfen dir, die für deinen Text passende Bedeutung zu finden.
- Die **Ziffern 1, 2** usw. zeigen, dass ein Stichwort unterschiedliche Bedeutungen haben oder unterschiedlichen Wortarten angehören kann (z. B. Adjektiv, Nomen, Verb).
- **Beispielsätze und Redewendungen** sind dem Stichwort zugeordnet.
- **Unregelmäßige Verbformen**, besondere **Pluralformen**, die **Steigerungsformen der Adjektive** und ähnliche Hinweise stehen oft in Klammern oder sind kursiv gedruckt.
- Die **Lautschrift** gibt Auskunft darüber, wie das Wort ausgesprochen und betont wird.

resort

resign /rɪˈzaɪn/
1 BERUF • *als Vorsitzender usw* zurücktreten: *He resigned from the company.* Er verließ das Unternehmen.
2 (*job, post*) aufgeben (*Stelle, Posten*)
3 **resign oneself to something** sich mit etwas abfinden
resignation /ˌrezɪɡˈneɪʃn/
1 BERUF • *bei Unternehmen* Kündigung; *von Minister usw* Rücktritt
2 **hand in one's resignation** *von Angestelltem* kündigen; *von Minister usw* sein Amt niederlegen
3 *Gemütszustand* Resignation
resigned /rɪˈzaɪnd/ (*look, sigh*) resigniert

resit[1] /ˌriːˈsɪt/ *Verb* (→ *sit*) *BE* (*exam*) wiederholen (*Prüfung*)
resit[2] /ˈriːsɪt/ *Substantiv* • *BE* Wiederholungsprüfung
resolution /ˌrezəˈluːʃn/
1 POLITIK Beschluss, Resolution
2 *bei Problem, Streit* Lösung
3 ≈ *Entschiedenheit* Entschlossenheit

TIPP: Wenn du ein Online-Wörterbuch verwenden möchtest, erkundige dich vorher bei deinem Lehrer/deiner Lehrerin, welche zu empfehlen sind, denn nicht alle sind gleich gut. Fast alle funktionieren aber nach den gleichen Prinzipien wie gedruckte Wörterbücher.

Einsprachige Wörterbücher

- Ein einsprachiges Wörterbuch erklärt die **Bedeutung** eines englischen Wortes **auf Englisch**. Da manche Wörter mehrere Bedeutungen haben, ist es wichtig, alle Einträge und Beispielsätze zu einem Wort zu lesen und mit deinem englischen Text zu vergleichen, um die korrekte Bedeutung herauszufinden.
- Das Wörterbuch hilft dir, die **passende Verbindung mit anderen Wörtern** zu finden, z. B. zu Verben, Präpositionen oder in bestimmten feststehenden Wendungen. Das ist nützlich, wenn du selbst einen englischen Text schreiben willst und nach den richtigen Wörtern suchst.

deadly ['dedli] *adj*
1 *able or likely to kill people* {= lethal}: This is no longer a deadly disease.
deadly to The HSN virus is deadly to chickens.
a deadly weapon The new generation of biological weapons is more deadly than ever.
2 *(only before noun)* {= complete}: ***deadly silence*** There was deadly silence after his speech.
a deadly secret Don't tell anyone – this is a deadly secret.
deadly serious *completely serious:* Don't laugh – I am deadly serious!
3 *(informal) very boring*: Many TV programmes are pretty deadly!

SF 38 Ordering and structuring vocabulary ➔ *SB (p. 134)*

Wortschatz strukturieren

Für das Ordnen von Wortschatz gibt es verschiedene Möglichkeiten. Du solltest unterschiedliche Formen ausprobieren und dann diejenige verwenden, die am besten zu dir passt. Es gibt z. B:
- Tabellen **(tables)**
- Diagramme (z. B. **tree diagrams**)
- Mindmaps

Wenn du Wortschatz zusammenstellst, solltest du daran denken, dass du für einen guten Text auch Varianten für Ausdrücke brauchst, die häufig vorkommen.

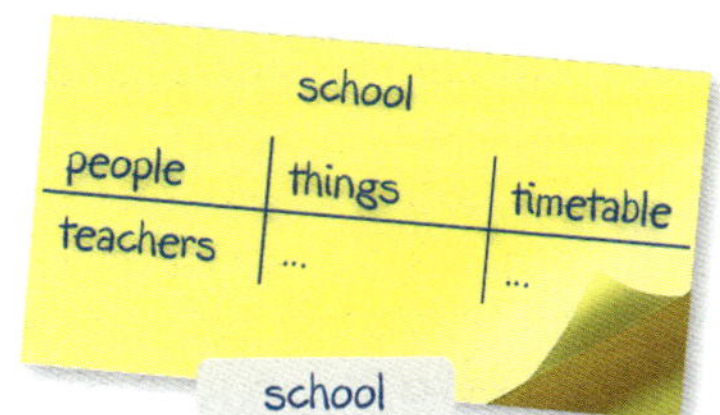

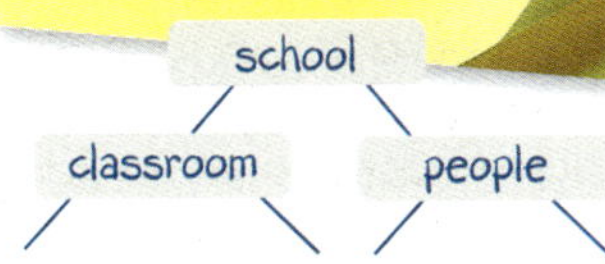

Wortschatz lernen und erweitern

Strukturierung eignet sich auch gut, um neue Wörter eines Wortfeldes zu lernen, da sich thematisch zusammenhängende Vokabeln leichter merken lassen. Damit kannst du deinen Wortschatz erweitern.

Eine gute Möglichkeit, thematisch zusammenhängenden Wortschatz zu lernen, ist, aus den Wörtern eines Wortfeldes eine Geschichte zu entwickeln und sie aufzuschreiben und evtl. passend zu illustrieren.

SF 39 Making and taking notes ➔ *SB (p. 134)*

Wenn du Informationen oder Gedanken kurz notierst – z. B. als Vorbereitung auf einen eigenen Vortrag oder eine Präsentation –, heißt das im Englischen **making notes**. Wenn du dir Notizen beim Lesen oder Zuhören machst, heißt das **taking notes**. Für beide Varianten gelten aber die gleichen Grundsätze.

Step 1: Achte auf **keywords**, die wichtige Informationen enthalten, um deine Frage zu beantworten oder den Inhalt eines Textes grob zu verstehen.

Step 2: Notiere nur die wichtigsten Informationen. Verwende **Abkürzungen und Symbole**, aber achte darauf, dass du ein System hast, damit du deine Notizen auch später noch verstehst. Markiere offene Fragen.

Step 3: Geh im Anschluss an das Lesen oder Hören nochmal durch deine Notizen und ergänze evtl. noch fehlende Informationen.

TIPP: Wenn du kein eigenes System von Abkürzungen hast, kannst du diese verwenden:

• the same as	=	• for example	*e. g.*
• not the same as	≠	• important	*!*
• about the same as	≈	• not	*x*
• and	+	• with	*w/*
• becomes/will be	->	• without	*w/o*
• between	*b/w*	• open question	*??*

SF 40 Preparing for a written exam ➔ *SB (pp. 135–137)*

Geschlossene Aufgaben

Vorbereitung

Step 1: Als erstes solltest du deine Lehrer fragen, welche Testformate möglicherweise vorkommen werden. Gängige geschlossene Aufgaben sind **multiple-choice tasks, true/false statements, matching tasks** und **gapped texts** (Lückentexte). Es kann sein, dass deine Prüfung nur ein Format enthält oder eine Mischung aus mehreren.

Step 2: Übe die unterschiedlichen Formate, z. B. mit dem Klassenarbeitstrainer oder frage deine Lehrerin/deinen Lehrer, ob sie/er Material hat. Mache dich mit den verschiedenen Formaten vertraut.

Durchführung

Step 1: Lies die Arbeitsanweisungen gut durch. Stelle sicher, dass du genau verstanden hast, was du tun sollst.

Step 2: Konzentriere dich auf die Informationen, die du benötigst, um die Aufgaben zu bearbeiten und mache dir Notizen dazu. (➔ *SF 39*)

- Bei **Höraufgaben** versuche so viel wie möglich beim ersten Hören zu verstehen und nutze das zweite Hören, um die Informationen zu vervollständigen. (➔ *SF 27*)
- Bei **Textaufgaben** lies den Text gründlich (wenn es um Details gehen soll) bzw. skimme/scanne ihn (wenn es um den groben Inhalt geht oder um bestimmte Informationen, (➔ *SF 1*)). Beantworte dann zuerst die Fragen, bei denen du dir sicher bist, und dann die, bei denen du länger nachdenken musst.
- Beantworte immer alle Aufgaben. Wenn du die Antwort nicht weißt, versuche die Antwort zu erschließen.

Hier sind noch einige Tipps, worauf du bei den einzelnen Testformaten besonders achten solltest:

Multiple-choice tasks

Bei *multiple-choice*-Aufgaben sollst du aus mehreren Antwortmöglichkeiten die korrekte auswählen.

- Lies die gegebenen Optionen sehr genau, denn manchmal sind Fallen darin versteckt: sie können z. B. Stichwörter aus dem Text enthalten, aber das genaue Gegenteil vom Textinhalt aussagen.
- Wenn du unsicher bist, was die richtige Antwort ist, gehe alle Antwortoptionen durch und überlege, warum sie falsch sein könnten.

True/false statements

Bei *true/false*-Aussagen geht es darum, jede gegebene Aussage hinsichtlich ihres Wahrheitsgehaltes zu überprüfen.

- Um falsche oder wahre Aussagen zu identifizieren, gehe durch den Text und finde Belege dafür. In der Regel kannst du Textstellen finden, die den Inhalt der Aussage widerspiegeln bzw. genau das Gegenteil sagen.
- Manchmal sollst du belegen, weshalb du eine Aussage für wahr oder falsch hältst. Nenne dann Textstellen, die du gefunden hast.

Matching tasks

Bei *matching*-Aufgaben werden Dinge einander zugeordnet, also z. B. Absätze und Überschriften oder Satzhälften.

- Ordne Dinge nicht einander zu, nur weil sie sich ähneln oder weil sie Wörter mit ähnlicher Bedeutung enthalten. Zur Sicherheit solltest du den Inhalt für dich umschreiben und nur Dinge mit passendem Inhalt einander zuordnen.

Gapped texts

Bei *gapped texts* müssen Lücken im Text sinnvoll befüllt werden.

- Achte besonders auf Wörter, die Sätze oder Gedanken verbinden wie z. B. *linking words* oder Pronomen sowie den Zeitablauf im Text. Diese Stellen können dir gute Hinweise geben, wie Lücken sinnvoll gefüllt werden sollten.
- Wenn du den Text vervollständigt hast, lies ihn nochmal gut durch, um sicher zu stellen, dass die Grammatik passt (Zeiten, Aktiv/Passiv etc.) und dass der Text logisch ist (kausale Zusammenhänge).

Offene Aufgaben

In den meisten Prüfungen wirst du mit Texten konfrontiert – dies können gedruckte Texte verschiedener **Textsorten** sein, aber auch visuelle Impulse wie Bilder, Cartoons oder Filmclips – oder mit Kombinationen von Texten wie z. B. ein Text und ein Bild, zu denen du Aufgaben bearbeiten sollst.

TIPP: Für die Bearbeitung dieser Aufgaben brauchst du unterschiedliche Techniken wie z. B.
- *skimming/scanning* (➔ *SF 1*)
- Texte markieren (➔ *SF 2*)
- Notizen machen (➔ *SF 39*)
- Texte schreiben (➔ *SF 3 ff.*).

Vorbereitung

Step 1: Erkundige dich, ob Hilfsmittel erlaubt sind (wie z. B. Wörterbücher).
Step 2: Übe mit alten Prüfungen, um zu sehen, was auf dich zukommen könnte.
Step 3: Lerne die wichtigsten Arbeitsanweisungen und was von dir dabei erwartet wird (siehe unten).

Durchführung

In der Regel werden die Aufgaben zum Text drei Anforderungsbereiche abdecken, zu denen du dich äußern musst. Diese Anforderungsbereiche sind:

- Anforderungsbereich I: Textverständnis
- Anforderungsbereich II: Analyse und Interpretation
- Anforderungsbereich III: Transfer

Die unterschiedlichen Anforderungsbereiche haben verschiedene Arbeitsanweisungen, an denen du sie erkennen kannst.

Im Folgenden kannst du sehen, was sie bedeuten und was von dir verlangt wird.

Anforderungsbereich I: Textverständnis

Diese Aufgaben befassen sich mit dem Inhalt des Textes. Hier sollst du zeigen, dass du den Text verstanden hast. Textverständnisaufgaben können entweder geschlossene Aufgaben sein (S. 135–136) oder offene Aufgaben.

Im Folgenden findest du Beispiele für typische Aufgaben zur Überprüfung des Textverständnisses. Wichtige Signalwörter für diesen Aufgabenbereich sind **outline, state sowie summarize/sum up/write a summary of**.

- Nenne die wichtigsten Punkte oder grundsätzliche Aspekte eines Themas:
  Outline the writer's views on … / Outline / Say why this topic is important.
- Erläutere einen bestimmten Punkt oder ein bestimmtes Thema im Text:
  State the authors opinion on …
- Gib eine knappe Darstellung eines Ereignisses oder Themas im Text oder fasse Inhalte des Textes knapp zusammen:
  Summarize the event described in the text in no more than four sentences. / Sum up the role of person X in this scene / Write a summary of …
- Es kann auch Kombinationen geben:
  Summarize the first scene and state why it is important for the rest of the text.

TIPP: Auf diese Dinge solltest du bei den einzelnen Arbeitsaufträgen achten:
- **outline:** Strukturiere deine Antwort in Haupt- und Unterpunkte (➔ *SF 6*)
- **state:** Sei präzise und finde Textstellen, die deine Meinung belegen
- **summarize:** Fasse dich kurz und gehe nicht ins Detail (➔ *SF 11*)

Anforderungsbereich II: Analyse/Interpretation

Bei diesen Aufgaben geht es um ein tieferes Verständnis des Textes, Hier sollst du zeigen, dass du nicht nur den Inhalt, sondern auch die Intention des Autors verstehst. Fragen, die du dir stellen solltest, sind z. B.: Warum hat der Autor etwas genau so beschrieben? Was will er/sie damit erreichen? An wen richtet sich der Text? Was sagt die Beschreibung eines Charakters über ihn/sie aus?

TIPP: Auf diese Dinge solltest du bei den einzelnen Arbeitsaufträgen achten:
- **analyse:** Stelle immer eine Verbindung zwischen verwendeten Stilmitteln und ihrer Wirkung her
- **examine:** Achte auf das, was im Text konkret steht ebenso wie auf Dinge, die sich „zwischen den Zeilen" befinden.
- **explain:** Beschreibe nicht nur, sondern begründe anhand des Textes, weshalb Dinge deiner Meinung nach so dargestellt sind, wie sie sind.

Es ist wichtig, die Arbeitsanweisungen genau zu lesen, damit du auch weißt, was von dir verlangt wird. Wichtige Signalwörter für diesen Aufgabenbereich sind **analyse, examine** oder **explain**:

- Beschreibe und erkläre bestimmte Aspekte eines Textes im Detail:
  Analyse the main elements of the poster/scene/text.
- Erläutere einen bestimmten Punkt oder ein bestimmtes Thema im Text:
  Examine the author's opinion of the main character.
- Beschreibe und definiere ein Ereignis/Thema oder einen bestimmten Punkt im Detail:
  Explain the main character's reaction to …

Anforderungsbereich III: Über den Text hinaus
Bei diesem dritten Teil bist du aufgefordert, selbst einen Text zu produzieren. Manchmal ist dir dabei die Textsorte freigestellt, manchmal ist eine bestimmte Textsorte vorgeschrieben.

Die Aufgabe kann auch darin bestehen, dich kreativ mit einem Text oder einem Thema auseinanderzusetzen, z. B. indem du ein Ende für einen Text oder eine Szene aus der Perspektive eines anderen Charakters schreiben sollst. Hier solltest du darauf achten, dass dein Stil zum Ausgangstext bzw. zu dem Charakter passt.

Beachte auf jeden Fall immer die Grundsätze für das Schreiben guter Texte. (➜ *SF 3 ff.*)

Im Folgenden findest du Beispiele für typische Aufgaben in diesem Anforderungsbereich. Wichtige Signalwörter in den Arbeitsaufträgen sind z. B. **comment on, discuss** oder **justify**.

- Gib deine Meinung zu einem Thema und begründe sie mit Belegen aus dem Text:
  Comment on the author's belief that … / Comment on the question of …
- Erörtere ein Thema. Bringe dabei Argumente pro und contra ein:
  Discuss why it is important for minorities to be represented in films/on TV.
- Finde Gründe und Belege für deine Meinung/Entscheidung/Schlussfolgerung:
  Justify your answer. / Justify why …

TIPP: Die Textsorten, die du in diesem Anforderungsbereich produzieren sollst, können z. B. sein:
- Artikel (➜ *SF 8*)
- Bericht (➜ *SF 10*)
- Kommentar (➜ *SF 9*)
- Erörterung (➜ *SF 7*)
- Brief/E-Mail (➜ *SF 13*)
- Review (➜ *SF 12*)

TIPP: Auf diese Dinge solltest du bei den einzelnen Arbeitsaufträgen achten:
- **comment on:** Bevor du schreibst, sammle Textbelege und strukturiere sie.
- **discuss:** Wäge beide Seiten des Themas ab und komme zu einer begründeten Schlussfolgerung.
- **justify:** Wenn möglich, unterstütze deine Position mit Textstellen.

SF 41 Preparing for a speaking exam ➜ *SB (pp. 138–139)*

Wie siwhr die Prüfung aus?

Step 1: Als erstes solltest du herausfinden, um welche Art von Prüfung es sich handelt. Es gibt zwei Formen: monologisches Sprechen oder dialogisches Sprechen (oder eine Kombination von beidem, z. B. zuerst ein Monolog, gefolgt von einem Dialog zu einem bestimmten Thema).

Monologisches Sprechen (p. 138)
- Präsentation/Mündlicher Vortrag als Reaktion auf einen Impuls
- Präsentation/Mündlicher Vortrag zu einem Thema (spontan oder vorbereitet)

Dialogisches Sprechen (p. 139)
- Gespräch mit einem Lehrer oder der Prüfungskommission
- Gespräch mit einer/m oder mehreren Partnern/Partnerinnen

Step 2: Informiere dich über weitere Aspekte:
- **Partner:** Kannst du eine/n Partner selbst wählen oder wird er/sie zugeteilt? Könnt ihr vor der Prüfung gemeinsam üben?
- **Format:** Welche Form hat die Prüfung? Freies Sprechen zu einem Thema oder bekommst du einen Impuls (Text, Bild etc.)?
- **Dauer:** Wie lange dauert die Prüfung/die einzelnen Teile?
- **Vorbereitung:** Wann erfährst du das Thema? Kannst du dich zu Hause vorbereiten oder erst direkt vor dem Test?
- **Medien:** Sollst du Medien (Computer, Folien etc) verwenden? Wieviel Zeit hast du, diese vorzubereiten?
- **Benotung:** Wie wird die Prüfung benotet? In der Regel setzt sich die Note aus Inhalt und sprachlicher Kompetenz zusammen.

Step 3: Sammle alle Informationen wie z. B. auch Musterprüfungen und Informationen zur Benotung in einem Ordner, so dass du schnell darauf Zugriff hast.

Monologisches Sprechen

Präsentation/mündlicher Vortrag zu einem Impuls

Wenn du in deinem mündlichen Vortrag auf einen Impuls reagieren sollst, kann das z. B. ein Bild oder Text sein, aber auch ein Zitat, eine Statistik, ein Cartoon oder eine oder mehrere Fragen. Oft erfährst du das erst kurz vor oder in der Prüfung selbst.

Aber auch wenn du nicht genau weißt, mit welcher Art von Impuls du konfrontierst wird, kannst du dich vorbereiten:

- Erstelle eine Mindmap oder Liste für jede Art von möglichem Impuls.
- Sammle darin Wörter oder ganze Sätze, um über die verschiedenen Impulse zu sprechen. Dies hilft dir, deinen Vortrag zu strukturieren, und deinem Gegenüber, ihm zu folgen. Lerne diese Redewendungen – wenn du sie sicher beherrschst, kannst du dich in der Prüfungssituation auf die Inhalte konzentrieren. (➜ *SF 18, SF 20, SF 31, SF 32*)

Präsentation/mündlicher Vortrag zu einem Thema

Wenn du für deine Prüfung eine Präsentation/einen mündlichen Vortrag zu einem Thema vorbereiten sollst, gehe dabei vor wie bei anderen Präsentationen auch (➜ *SF 21*). Einige Punkte solltest du aber besonders beachten:

- **Struktur:** Stelle sicher, dass die Zuhörer deiner Präsentation gut folgen können. Lerne und verwende Redewendungen wie *first of all, finally, next, I would like to finish by saying …*
- **Medien:** Bereite alle Medien (Bilder, Präsentationen etc.) gut vor. Dazu gehören z. B. auch deine Notizen, am besten auf Karteikarten.
- **Zeitmanagement:** Halte dich an die vorgegebene Zeit. Das schaffst du am besten, wenn du deine Präsentation ein paar Mal laut übst, z. B. vor einem Partner/einer Partnerin oder deiner Familie.
- **Vortrag:** Sieh die Prüfer an, wenn du sprichst, nicht deine Notizen. Sprich langsam, deutlich und lass dir ruhig Zeit, zwischendurch mal tief Luft zu holen, besonders wenn du nervös bist. Mach das auch schon beim Üben.

Dialoge – an Gesprächen teilnehmen

Oft beinhaltet eine mündliche Prüfung auch einen dialogischen Teil, in dem du mit einem Partner oder den Prüfern kommunizierst.

Dies kann z. B. ein Gespräch zu einem Thema sein, aber auch eine Diskussion, ein Interview oder ein Rollenspiel. Auch wenn du nicht genau weißt, mit was du in der Prüfung konfrontierst wird, kannst du dich auf die Situation vorbereiten.

Step 1: Überlege dir, evtl. mit einem Partner/einer Partnerin, im Vorfeld für jede der möglichen Formen – Gespräch, Diskussion, Interview, Rollenspiel – worauf du dabei achten musst.

Step 2: Notiere dir, was du an Phrasen und Redewendungen für die einzelnen Phasen eines Dialoges brauchst und lerne sie. (➜ *SF 18, SF 20*)

- **Anfang einer Diskussion:**
  Today we're talking about … / Let me start with … / …
- **Zustimmen/widersprechen:**
  What a great/… idea. / My point exactly. / … That's not how I see it. / I don't agree with …
- **Nachfragen:**
  Can you give an example of that? / Do you mean …?
- **Eine/n Partner/in einbeziehen:**
  How about you? / What do you think / How do you feel about that?
- **Unterbrechen:**
  May I interrupt? / Excuse me, can I just say that …?
- **Zeit zum Überlegen gewinnen:**
  Can I repeat what we said before? / Well, now let me see … / Let me think about that for a second.
- **Zusammenfassen:**
  We've seen that … / To come to a conclusion …

TIPP: Beachte auch diese allgemeinen Tipps für die Prüfungssituation:

- Erstelle deine Notizen so, dass du sie schnell finden und auf einen Blick entziffern kannst.
- Sei gut ausgeschlafen. Trage angemessene Kleidung, in der du dich auch wohlfühlst. Sei pünktlich.
- Sei höflich und freundlich. Bedenke auch, dass du in einer dialogischen Prüfungssituation nicht für deine eigene Note arbeitest, sondern auch für deine/n Partner/in.

Checkpoint 1

1 WORDS A profile

2 huge 3 absolutely 4 fairly 5 particularly 6 conventional 7 quite 8 influenced 9 extremely 10 ambitious 11 lot 12 very 13 passionate 14 great 15 musical 16 not 17 especially

2 Why is he being photographed?

2 Why are the scientists being arrested? 3 Why is her car being stopped? 4 Where is the device being taken? 5 Why is that woman being watched? 6 How is the information being sent?

3 Writing an opinion piece: language structures

a) 1 ✔ 3 ✔

b) 1 mustn't 2 ought to 3 should 4 can 5 has to 6 must

4 Writing an opinion piece: tips for Maddison

- You should make the first paragraph short.
- State your opinion and topic clearly in the first paragraph.
- You should use things like quotes and statistics to back up your main statement.
- Include the personal pronouns **I**, **you** and **we**: e. g., **I** shows how strongly you feel.
- Tell anecdotes about things that have happened to you.
- Use less well-known facts to surprise your reader.
- Use rhetorical questions to say things in a more emphatic way.
- Let me read it when you have finished!

5 Money and identity: writing an opinion piece

a) **Follow the guidelines for writing an opinion piece. Ideas:**
- being afraid of not having enough money or losing it
- not having enough money → being afraid of living in need, thinking: more money can change the situation → influence our thoughts/identity
- not spending a lot: (1) positive: people don't focus on material things; (2) negative: people see themselves and others as losers
- spending/not spending money: influences our emotions → success? failing?
- Are my personal strengths connected to money?

b) **Ideas:**
- advertisements: everywhere (on TV, online, at the cinema, in magazines, on the street, in shop windows), big business
- the newest object: we = happy, the 'right' kind of life → wrong
- our value as people ≠ the things we own
- Jonathan Swift: A wise person should have money in their head, but not in their heart.
- adverts
  - influence us: the problem is that we want the things we see in adverts and we feel bad if we don't get them
  - appeal to our emotions instead of using facts
- some people: afraid of being laughed at if they don't have the latest clothes → importance of money, shopping, technical devices, etc.
- attack our self-confidence → our identity is linked to what we can and cannot buy
- extremely difficult situation for young people who are trying to find their place in the world
- solution: limit the number of adverts by law, don't allow companies to make any adverts for children
- better: focus on human beings and relationships

Checkpoint 2

1 We do need to take action

1 Young people do need to start campaigning.
It's young people who need to start campaigning.
Young people need to start campaigning themselves.
Young people definitely need to start campaigning.

2 My MP does get involved in local projects.
It's my MP who gets involved in local projects /
It's local projects that my MP gets involved in.
My MP gets involved in local projects herself/himself.
My MP really gets involved in local projects.

2 *Boxes of Hope*: a community project

1 of feeling 2 of doing 3 of starting 4 in being 5 on receiving 6 of making 7 in giving 8 of bringing

3 The European Parliament in Brussels

a) **Text 1:** include plenaries and committee meetings
Text 3: the European Parliament's visitor centre / in the Parliament's Espace Leopold complex in Brussels / There's no need to book

b) 1 **Text 1:** you can watch all public events online/streaming
2 **Text 3:** Visits don't cost a cent

4 *Step Inside*: helping people back …

a) 1 The clothes sold in the shop are different because they are used. 2 It was a good idea to start a shop because people often give clothes to the organization, but the organization can't use everything. 3 The location is a nice area with lovely shops. 4 The students who helped Phil took photos, then they were allowed to use the photos for their college design project, and they got very good marks. 5 This year, the charity has helped nearly 800 people to get a job again. 6 People in the area like the shop because they can take clothes there and know that they are helping the charity.

b) *l. 1:* boutique – Boutique *l. 4:* brainchild – Idee, Einfall *l. 6:* to sleep rough – im Freien übernachten (obdachlos sein) *l. 8:* donation – Spende *l. 9:* item – Artikel, Gegenstand *l. 16:* marvellous – großartig, wunderbar *l. 19:* customer – Kunde/Kundin *l. 21:* to benefit – profitieren *l. 28:* to invest – investieren

c) **Step Inside:** sells used clothes / team of volunteers / money that they make → *The Dale Centre* / organization: gives homeless people somewhere to sleep in the winter / helps them to find work and a place to live / some: work in the shop to get experience / get clothes from the shop for job interviews / successful project

d) I would buy used clothes from this shop or a similar one: good idea, using old clothes again → good for the environment / cheaper than buying new clothes all the time

Checkpoint 3

1 PRONUNCIATION Word stress

1 alternative 2 battery 3 complex 4 controversial
5 digital 6 electricity 7 exclusive 8 an export
9 to export 10 parasite 11 radioactive 12 vision

2 WORDS Defining words

a) 2 to hesitate 3 to charge 4 to replace

b) 2 to bring something to someone 's house 3 to relax
4 to know what's going to happen

3 Using adverbs

2 New species mean that we can use resources more economically. 3 Luckily the patient recovered completely. 4 We only vaguely understand the threat this issue might cause. 5 Could you please explain concisely what the issue is exactly? 6 I sincerely hope we can come to an agreement on this matter.

4 Presenting your opinion in a panel discussion

a) 2 You can't just say that without giving an explanation.
3 I think this is the best idea to proceed. / the problem isn't just going to go away. / this needs to be done immediately.
4 In my opinion, this is the best idea to proceed. / the problem isn't just going to go away. / this needs to be done immediately.
5 I don't think we've got any new ideas. 6 As we have seen, this is the best idea to proceed. / the problem isn't just going to go away. / this needs to be done immediately.

b) 2 I don't think so. The problem is that the plastic will never go away. 3 I agree, the sea is huge, but we are filling it with rubbish. 4 In my opinion, plastic is just as dangerous as radioactive waste. 5 I don't think it's that easy, because it just stays in the water in tiny pieces. 6 You can't say it won't affect your children. It already does.

c)
- be well-prepared
- write down your own arguments and think about what arguments the others might present
- present a short statement at the beginning
- remember to listen to others

Ideas:
- water pollution: kills fish and kills us
- controlling air pollution for years, but what have we been doing with water?
- filling it more and more with our rubbish: plastic shopping bags
- plastic bags don't just 'disappear'
- US Ocean Service: huge regions with plastic forming a kind of soup
- birds and fish eat that 'soup' → animals: dying
- lots of them = our food
- beaches covered in tins, plastic bags, etc.
- Who wants to go on holiday and swim in a sea full of rubbish?
- worse: soup will not go away
- stop throwing plastic in the sea → the plastic that is there will not disappear → clean it up → not simple
- plans to clean sea
- governments: need to work together, help keep our seas safe for the future
- Keeping our planet clean starts with us, at home.
- think before you want to buy something with lots of plastic
- recycle, reuse glass bottles → better for the environment
- We've only got one planet.

Tonaufnahmen
Tonstudio: Clarity Studio Berlin
Regie und Aufnahmeleitung: Gareth Evans, Susanne Kreuzer
Tontechnik: Hüseyin Dönertaş, Christian Marx, Christian Schmitz, Pascal Thinius
Sprecher/Innen: Denis Abrahams, Gareth Evans, Roman Hemetsberger, Jeffrey Mittleman, Kim Pfeiffer, Melina Rost, Darren Smith, Tomas Spencer, Joshua Spriggs, Clare Wigfall, Laura Wilkinson, Ian Wood

Titelbild: Junge Frau [M]: Shutterstock/lzf; Landstraße [M]: Glowimages

Illustrationen: Christian Bartz, Berlin; S. 56, 58, 60, 62, 64, 66, 68, 70, 72, 74, 76, 78/Nussschale: Roland Beier; S. 74: Doreen Arnold

Bildquellen: Klappe/Junge: Shutterstock/HBRH; Klappe/Gruppe: Shutterstock/Monkey Business Images; Klappe/Windrad: Shutterstock/Bildagentur Zoonar Gmbh; S. 2/Bild 1: Shutterstock/HBRH; S. 2/Bild 2: Shutterstock/mimagephotography; S. 4/li.: Shutterstock/Atelier KNOX; S. 4/re.: Shutterstock/Liyba Dozz; S. 5/ob.: Shutterstock/Undrey; S. 5/un.: Shutterstock/panitanphoto; S. 6: Shutterstock/Neale Cousland; S. 7/ob.: Shutterstock/George Rudy; S. 7/un.: Shutterstock/Nestyda; S. 8: Shutterstock/Ollyy; S. 9/Bild 1: Shutterstock/Maxisport; S. 9/Bild 2: Shutterstock/Aprilphoto; S. 9/Bild 3: Shutterstock/Hadrian; S. 9/Bild 4: Shutterstock/Felipe Junqueira Borges; S. 9/Bild 5: Shutterstock/Ladanivskyy Oleksandr; S. 10: Shutterstock/Asvolas; S. 11: Shutterstock/I'm Friday; S. 12: Shutterstock/FXQuadro; S. 13: Shutterstock/sirtravelalot; S. 15: Shutterstock/BENCHAMAT; S. 16/Bild 1: Shutterstock/Monkey Business Images; S16/Bild 2: Shutterstock/Pavel L Photo and Video; S. 16/Bild 3: Shutterstock/adriaticfoto; S. 16/Bild 4: Shutterstock/Jacob Lund; S. 17: Shutterstock/Aaron Amat; S. 18: Shutterstock/Carlos E. Santa Maria; S. 19: Shutterstock/Africa Studio; S. 20/ob.: Shutterstock/Labrador Photo Video; S. 20/un. li.: Shutterstock/mangostock; S. 20/un. re.: Shutterstock/Syda Productions; S. 22: Shutterstock/Artem Oleshko; S. 23: Shutterstock/Vanatchanan; S. 24/ob.: Shutterstock/Samuel Borges Photography; S. 24/mi.: Shutterstock/Sergey Furtaev; S. 24/un.: Shutterstock/Pressurepics; S. 25/ob.: Shutterstock/Armin Staudt; S. 25/un.: Shutterstock/Photographee.eu; S. 26: Shutterstock/symbiot; S. 27: Shutterstock/S_L; S. 28/ob. li.: Shutterstock/Sergmam; S. 28/ob. re.: Shutterstock/irma thea marren; S. 28/un. li.: Shutterstock/Ruth Black; S. 28/un. re.: Shutterstock/matka_Wariatka; S. 29: Shutterstock/Npeter; S. 30/Bild 1: Shutterstock/Davizro Photography; S. 30/Bild 2: Shutterstock/Sentavio; S. 34: Shutterstock/Rawpixel.com; S. 35: Shutterstock/Dalshe; S. 37/li.: Shutterstock/Bildagentur Zoonar Gmb; S. 37/mi.: Shutterstock/Diyana Dimitrova; S. 37/re.: Shutterstock/stocksolutions; S. 39: Shutterstock/Monkey Business Images; S. 41/li.: Shutterstock/Daren Woodward; S. 41/re.: Fotolia/Richard Carey; S. 45: Shutterstock/sylv1rob1; S. 46 shutterstock/razorbeam; S. 47: Shutterstock/Syda Productions; S. 48: Shutterstock/Ridkous Mykhailo; S. 49: Shutterstock/Aleutie; S. 50: Shutterstock/Rawpixel.com; S. 51: Shutterstock/venimo; S. 52/li.: Shutterstock/Daisy Daisy; S. 52/mi.: Shutterstock/Josep Suria; S. 52/re.: Shutterstock/Denys Prykhodov; S. 53: Shutterstock/Dima Sidelnikov; S. 54: Shutterstock/Tyler Olson; S. 56/ob.: Shutterstock/sarahdesign; S. 56/un.: Shutterstock/AVAVA; S. 58/Wordle: Cornelsen/Bonnie Glänzer; S. 59: Fotolia/structuresxx; S. 63/ob.: Cornelsen/Bonnie Glänzer; S. 63/un.: Fotolia/undrey; S. 64, 67: Sapna Richter, Berlin; S. 68/ob.: Fotolia/luzitanija: S. 68/un.: Mauritius images/Alamy/Picture Partners; S. 69/ob.: Fotolia/Miriam Dörr; S. 69/2. v. ob.: Cornelsen Verlag/Crooked Letter Films, NY; S. 69/2. v. un.: Cornelsen Verlag/Crooked Letter Films, NY; S. 69/un.: Cornelsen Verlag/Crooked Letter Films, NY; S. 71: Sapna Richter, Berlin; S. 72: Shutterstock/Cartoonresource; S. 73: Fotolia/Rawpixel.com; S. 74/ob.: Cornelsen; S. 74/un.: Shutterstock/kanate